MW01154834

Grave Expectations on Dickens' Dune

Seaview Cottages Cozy Mystery #3

Anna Celeste Burke

GRAVE EXPECTATIONS ON DICKENS' DUNE
Copyright © 2019 Anna Celeste Burke
desertcitiesmystery.com
Independently Published

All rights reserved. No part of this work may be reproduced without written permission of the publisher except brief quotations for review purposes.

This is a work of fiction. Names, characters, businesses, places, events and incidents are either the products of the author's imagination or used in a fictitious manner. Any resemblance to actual persons, living or dead, or actual events is purely coincidental.

Cover Design by Anna Celeste Burke
Photo © Miraswonderland | Dreamstime.com and © Jo Ann Snover | Dreamstime.com

Books by USA Today and Wall Street Journal Bestselling Author Anna Celeste Burke

A Dead Husband Jessica Huntington Desert Cities Mystery #1

A Dead Sister Jessica Huntington Desert Cities Mystery #2

A Dead Daughter Jessica Huntington Desert Cities Mystery # 3

A Dead Mother Jessica Huntington Desert Cities Mystery #4

A Dead Cousin Jessica Huntington Desert Cities Mystery #5

A Dead Nephew Jessica Huntington Desert Cities Mystery #6 [2019]

Love A Foot Above the Ground Prequel to the Jessica Huntington Desert Cities Mystery Series

Cowabunga Christmas! Corsario Cove Cozy Mystery #1

Gnarly New Year! Corsario Cove Cozy Mystery #2

Heinous Habits! Corsario Cove Cozy Mystery #3

Radical Regatta! Corsario Cove Cozy Mystery #4 for preorder now in Summer Snoops Unleashed: 14 Furr-ocious Mysteries and Cozy Crimes. Available as a standalone in November 2019.

Murder at Catmmando Mountain Georgie Shaw Cozy Mystery #1

Love Notes in the Key of Sea Georgie Shaw Cozy Mystery #2
All Hallows' Eve Heist Georgie Shaw Cozy Mystery #3
A Merry Christmas Wedding Mystery Georgie Shaw Cozy Mystery #4
Murder at Sea of Passenger X Georgie Shaw Cozy Mystery #5
Murder of the Maestro Georgie Shaw Cozy Mystery #6
A Tango Before Dying Georgie Shaw Cozy Mystery #7
A Canary in the Canal Georgie Shaw Cozy Mystery #8 [2019]

A Body on Fitzgerald's Bluff Seaview Cottages Cozy Mystery #1
The Murder of Shakespeare's Ghost Seaview Cottages Cozy Mystery #2
Grave Expectations on Dickens' Dune Seaview Cottages Cozy Mystery #3

Lily's Homecoming Under Fire Calla Lily Mystery #1
Tangled Vines, Buried Secrets Calla Lily Mystery #2 [2019]

DEDICATION

To Charles Dickens' wishes for us all: a heart that never hardens and a yielding spirit that when bent and broken takes on a better shape.

Contents

ACKNOWLEDGMENTS

This book, like all the others, could not have been written without my husband's input and support. I ask him dozens of questions while I'm writing, ranging from big issues about how to resolve a plot dilemma to small ones like the choice of which word to use in a sentence. He's always helpful, supportive, and patient. Thank you!

Thanks to my wonderful editor, Peggy Hyndman who tackles the first round of editing on the manuscript with a directness I appreciate, with thoroughness, and amazing speed. I'll never know how she does all that she does for me and so many other authors fortunate enough to have her support.

I'm also grateful to Ying Cooper for her input on this manuscript. She never lets me get away with a thing—checks the references to famous people, places, songs, and books. She finds the sneakiest missing word and even extra spaces that slip in.

Acknowledgments would never be complete without thanking my readers for their ongoing support. That's especially true for my "ARC Angels" who read imperfect versions of my books before Peggy & Ying get to them. I'm blessed to have their feedback and I'm grateful for their support.

A special thanks to Judith Rogow for lending her name to an imaginary character in this story.

CAST OF CHARACTERS

Dear reader, if you'd prefer to be surprised as each character is introduced please skip this section!

GRAND OLD LADY DETECTIVES:

Miriam Webster, who lives in Hemingway Cottage, was a bookkeeper, is a talented baker, and her fur baby is a Dalmatian, named Domino.

Penelope Parker lives in Brontë Cottage, is a member of the Seaview Cottages Walkers Club, and has a Jack Russell Terrier, named Emily. Penelope prefers to be called Charly in honor of her favorite writer, Charlotte Brontë, and is a retired criminology professor.

Cornelia "Neely" Conrad lives in Christie Cottage and is a self-proclaimed night owl who loves to read. Neely is retired and was an actress, turned costume designer and makeup artist.

Marty Monroe lives in Fitzgerald Cottage and is a member of the Seaview Cottages Walkers Club. Before retiring, Marty spent decades working as a buyer for high-end department stores.

Midge Gaylord lives in Austen Cottage and is a member of the Seaview Cottages Walkers Club. Midge is an ex-Army trauma care nurse, with ties to the local medical community.

OTHER SEAVIEW COTTAGES RESIDENTS AND EMPLOYEES:

Carl Rodgers lives in Steinbeck Cottage and is the former manager of a collection agency.

Joe Torrance, who lives in Chandler Cottage, is a retired auto dealership service manager and mechanic.

Greta Bishop lives in the Garbo Cottage. She used to be the resident Realtor and a Seaview Cottages HOA board member until legal issues led to her resignation.

Robyn Chappell is dating Joe Torrance. She lived in the Shakespeare Cottage and just purchased the du Maurier Cottage.

Alyssa Gardner and her husband who live in the Potter Cottage are snooty residents at the center of lots of gossip in the community.

LAW ENFORCEMENT:

Darnell Devers is a Deputy Sheriff for whom the locals have various pet names due to his "do as little as possible attitude."

Henry "Hank" Miller is the personable and competent lead detective with the County Sheriff's Department. Assigned to the Criminal Investigations Bureau, he and his colleagues are tasked with investigations of major crimes against persons and property.

Eddie Vargas was a detective from outside the local area who worked with Hank Miller on a case related to the trouble at Shakespeare Cottage.

Officer Denver Clemons is an officer with the County Sheriff's Department who works undercover.

Harold is Charly's friend and an investigator from the U.S. Treasury Department.

SECONDARY CHARACTERS:

Judith Rogow is Charly Parker's friend. She hires G.O.L.D. to solve the mystery of her ex-husband's disappearance and alleged murder—a cold case that's decades old.

Allen Rogow is Judith Rogow's ex-husband who police suspected had met with foul play on Dickens' Dune. The case went cold when they never found his body.

Leonard Cohen is an ex-convict who makes a startling deathbed confession.

Wendy Ballard is a young woman who Allen Rogow met in drug treatment.

Nick Martinique is a friend of Wendy Ballard's who also has drug problems.

Chelsea Glen is Neely's friend and contact at the resort in Pismo Beach.

Elizabeth Stockton is the nurse at the hospital to whom Leonard Cohen made his deathbed confession.

Ginger Winger is Leonard Cohen's ex-wife.

Jimmy Dunn is an acquaintance Miriam's husband, Peter Webster, knew before he died.

Ricardo Cantinela is a high-powered lawyer.

Mark Viceroy is an Army buddy who served with Allen Rogow during the Vietnam War.

1

Grave Matters

"There's more of gravy than of grave about you, whatever you are!"
—A Christmas Carol

∞

GRAVE HUNTING IS no job for a woman on her own. Not that I was entirely alone. Domino, my Dalmatian, was with me. At almost a year old, she's a sensitive creature, sweet and friendly, and far more alert to signals that something's not right than I am. When she began to whine anxiously, I should have turned back.

Dickens' Dune beckoned, however, and my curiosity drove me on oblivious to Domino's initial wariness. Rising out of the sand the hill ahead towered over the surrounding scrubby bluffs, rolling dunes, and sandy beach beyond. Although everyone refers to it as Dickens' Dune, it isn't a dune at all. It's an outcropping of rocky granite deposited along California's Central Coast during some ancient movement of a receding glacier. Over the years, sand had covered the rocky surface completely, giving it the appearance of a super-sized dune on the side facing the Pacific

Ocean.

As Domino and I drew closer, the looming hillside cast shadows on the trail we'd taken from the parking lot at the entrance to Dickens' Dune Seaside Park. At seven in the morning on a weekday, the lot had been almost empty. A car had pulled in not long after I did which wasn't at all unusual. Summer visitors would begin to fill the lot as they roused themselves to start a lazy vacation day along this gorgeous stretch of the blue Pacific Ocean. The gulls were already awake and screamed overhead.

When we were close enough that the shadows from Dickens' Dune engulfed us, the trail split. The path ahead continued down to the beach. A breeze rippled on the frothy waves as they rolled into shore, causing sunlight to sparkle as it skittered across the surface of the water. I breathed in the salty air, relishing the potpourri of scents that had become familiar since Domino and I moved here. The citrusy fragrance of pale lavender verbena blooms dominated the heady mix of scents this morning.

Off to my left, the path wandered for miles through the sandy expanse of dunes back to the beachfront cottages crammed full of summer guests on California's so-called "American Riviera." The area around here isn't as glamorous as Santa Barbara, which is farther down the coast. Most of the beachfront cottages are even older than the ones in our Seaview Cottages active adult community that sits across the roadway and up above on high bluffs overlooking the ocean.

Our cottages are comfy but modest, especially in comparison to The Blue Haven Resort and Spa a few miles south of us that aspires to the grandeur befitting an

American Riviera. Pricewise, they've achieved their aspirations. On my right, the path inclined upward as it wound around behind Dickens' Dune. That's where Domino and I were headed. I hesitated for a moment at the prospect that the trail led to the scene of a murder.

"If Leonard Cohen's deathbed confession can be trusted, Domino, all that happened decades ago, though, right?" Domino woofed, although she didn't pull me ahead as she often does on our walks along more familiar trails. A sign posted nearby reminded us to stay on the trail which, here on the backside of Dickens' Dune, was a narrow rocky ridge climb with lots of switchbacks. "Let's go, girl. If we can locate that old bunker, that'll be enough for today."

Domino woofed again and took off, yanking me forward. The trail's incline soon had me breathing hard at the pace we set, despite the loose gravel underfoot which I'd slipped on twice. When I'd lost my footing, Domino had done her worried, clumsy-human check, slowing and anxiously looking over her shoulder. She picked up the pace once I reassured her that I was okay.

Fifteen minutes later, after negotiating another switchback on the zigzag trail, a quick look down the slope below revealed how much elevation we'd gained. As I raised a water bottle to my lips, I glimpsed movement in the parking lot. Standing beside a car, a man scanned the hillside with a pair of binoculars. The hair on my arms stood up when his exploration of the area stopped. I could have sworn his gaze was fixed on us.

Domino must have sensed my discomfort and stepped closer to me. She growled and then barked. Maybe he heard her or realized I was staring at him. In any case, he focused his binoculars onto the trail that led back toward the summer cottages. When he waved an arm in that direction, I breathed a sigh of relief. From my higher vantage point, though, I couldn't see a soul anywhere on that leg of the trail. When I shifted my gaze back to the parking lot, the car was still there, but the voyeur with the binoculars was gone. Perhaps the person he was waving at had parked in another lot and wasn't on the trail at all but closer to him.

"Come on! Your Momma's becoming paranoid in her old age. I do have my reasons, though, don't I?" Domino wagged her tail and nuzzled my palm, which I took to mean she agreed with me. A dead husband's secrets and two recent episodes of murder and mayhem had taken a toll on my Midwestern predisposition to believe in the trustworthiness of the people I met.

"Where do you suppose that guy went?" I muttered as I took one last glance over my shoulder while moving up the trail again. "You know what, Domino? We'll get the best views of what's going on below from the summit of Dickens' Dune. Are you game to go all the way to the top?" She didn't stop but woofed and wagged her tail. I hadn't planned to climb to that point so I couldn't remember how much farther the summit was from the abandoned bunker.

At the next switchback, I searched and glimpsed a dark hollow in the rock above us. A little too regular in shape to be Mother Nature's doing, it must be the site of the old observation point that had been cut into Dickens' Dune. At one of the highest elevations along this part of California's Central Coast, it had been built during World War II and was used as a lookout for Japanese ships and submarines.

A small slit on the front side of the hillside was virtually invisible from offshore or the beach below. Soldiers, on duty twenty-four/seven, kept watch. If they spotted a ship, they'd signal their colleagues. Fitted with a battery of big guns at an artillery post overlooking the Pacific Ocean from a promontory near Steinbeck's Cove, it was their job to prevent intruders from moving north to the San Francisco Bay Area or sending anyone ashore. The guns were all that remained and were on display in a memorial near the cove.

"What do you think of this?" I asked Domino when we reached the bunker about ten minutes later. I had to restrain my curious pooch, who would willingly have tried to slip under or through the gates that prevented access to the open bunker. She whined and whimpered as she strained against my hold on her leash.

"No, Domino, we're not welcome. How about a treat?" I asked as I slipped a baggie from the fanny pack I wore. Domino's a sucker for my homemade peanut butter doggie biscuits and scarfed it down in the blink of an eye. I poured water into the hollow of a nearby boulder, and she lapped it up while I examined the area, trying to view it in the context of the circumstances that had sent me here this morning.

Judith Rogow, a new client, had hired us to investigate her ex-husband's disappearance in the early 1980s. She'd recently been told that Allen Rogow was murdered and buried somewhere on Dickens' Dune. As soon as I'd begun to snoop, the old bunker jumped out at me as a place where Allen Rogow's killer could have done the deed without being observed. There were plenty of places nearby to conceal a body. Shivers slid up my spine as I imagined the hollow eyes of a skull peering at me from remains hidden between boulders.

While it was off limits now, the bunker had still been open when Allen Rogow vanished. From what I'd read it was sometimes used as a hangout for hikers during the day back then. At night, most of the visitors were local high school kids who used the place to hide and smoke or drink. Drugs changed all that, though, and after several unsavory incidents, the drumbeat began to sound, urging authorities to close off access. In the mid-eighties, the gates went up, along with the no trespass signs.

A stream of light illuminated the interior. That had to be coming from the opening facing the ocean, which the soldiers had used during their watch. What I could see of the interior from the helter-skelter lighting conformed to the pictures I'd found online. Cement walls marked with graffiti surrounded a cracked cement floor littered with dirt and debris. In places, the cement had begun to crumble and had become part of the litter.

Most of the graffiti that I could read was initials, but a few words were scrawled here and there. Some of it was crude and reminiscent of the stuff I'd seen on bathroom stalls when I was much younger. There were odd ramblings and symbols like the all-seeing eye inside a pyramid, a lightning bolt, hearts, and stick people. Perhaps they were related to popular songs or slang that was too dated or too hip for me to recognize. They also called to mind photos I'd seen of cave paintings or petroglyphs.

I tried not to look too closely at the disgusting mix of cigarette butts, beer bottle caps, fast food wrappers, and castoff clothing that was strewn about on the floor. A filthy old cushion like a camper might use under a sleeping bag or on a cot was leaning on its side in one corner. It was hard to imagine hanging out in there. Even harder to conceive of anyone camping out overnight or, heaven forbid, staying in the bunker for longer than that. I felt claustrophobic just looking at the space. As my inner sleuth perked up, I could envision it as a place to hold someone against his will, although not for long with teens nosing around.

Judith hadn't told us why Allen Rogow was anywhere near Dickens' Dune. The abandoned bunker could have served as a private meeting place, if the murder was premeditated and someone had lured Allen Rogow to his death. I closed my eyes, but I could still see the stains on the cement floor and on that cushion. The police claimed to have found signs of foul play somewhere on Dickens' Dune—did they mean inside the bunker?

No one had ever found Allen Rogow's body. The sound of the ocean waves below was a reminder that he wouldn't have been the first dead man—or woman as my group of sleuthing friends and I had recently learned—to be dumped into a watery grave. A cold, clammy breeze swirled around my head and neck, leaving a tingle on my scalp. Domino and I both jumped at what sounded like boots on gravel.

Had the man with the binoculars caught up with us? I wondered as I looked around for a place to hide. He'd given me no cause to run or hide, but my preoccupation with matters of the grave had me eager to get away. I gave Domino's leash a tug and then bolted up the trail toward the summit.

I paused to scan the trail below, but I couldn't see anyone. There were more footsteps, and that got me moving again. We hadn't gone far when I suddenly heard coughing, followed by words I couldn't make out, and laughter. It was a woman's laugh. I slowed down and allowed my breathing to ease up. That's when I recalled a few words from the little of Dickens' work with which I'm familiar.

"*There's more of gravy than of grave about you, whatever you are!*" In my case, "whoever you are" was more appropriate since it was a person and not a specter that had spooked me. Meeting another hiker on a public trail in broad daylight was no reason for alarm. Unlike Scrooge, I couldn't blame my irrational fear on gravy or a bit of undigested meat since that wasn't part of my breakfast.

"Not a spook or a cutthroat, but a lesson learned," I said aloud. "No more grave hunting alone." To my surprise, Domino uttered a low guttural sound which got me climbing again. We didn't stop until we reached a set of steps cut into the rock that led to the summit of Dickens' Dune. At the top of those steps, the view was spectacular. Dizzying too, when I inched my way to the edge and looked down to see if I could catch a glimpse of who was on the trail below us.

A bit of gravel slid off the side, and the male member of the couple below glanced up and made eye contact with me. A smile formed on his lips. As paranoia gripped me again, it appeared to me as a sly "gotcha" kind of smile. I stepped back from the precipice, trying to calm my beating heart and tame my wild imagination.

I also quickly searched for another way down from here. I reached into my pocket where I carry a self-defense keychain weapon called a kubotan. It was quite useful, although the summit of Dickens' Dune was an unfortunate place to have to take a stand. I searched again and spotted what appeared to be an old, abandoned trail. There weren't any steps cut into the hillside where Domino and I stood, and the shadows made it hard to tell how far a drop it was to the ground below.

Footsteps crunching on the rocky trail were closer now. I turned to face the point at which we'd stepped onto the summit, and braced myself for a confrontation. "Think, Miriam, think!" I muttered aloud. I'd seen the man before, but where? No good association popped into my mind as I struggled to recall who he could be, just a sick, uneasy feeling.

Surely, we couldn't have stirred up old trouble related to Allen Rogow's death already, had we? Our investigation had barely begun. Had I met the man during one of the murder investigations that my friends and I had recently been mixed up in? Nothing registered.

I pulled Domino closer as a new question formed, displacing my efforts to recall where I'd seen the man before. How did he know I'd be here this morning? He must have followed me. With that possibility looming, I heard those footsteps moving more quickly, accompanied by a hacking cough.

"Let's go!" I whispered. "Momma first." I eased

backward off the ledge and my feet touched the ground with no trouble. Domino followed, and we moved as quickly as we could, using the remnants of makeshift steps, slipping and sliding as we fled. I looked over my shoulder and didn't see anyone coming after us. Soon, the old trail became easier to follow, although our descent was angled on a steeper decline.

I continued to slip and slide on the loose gravel that had accumulated on the unkempt trail, but we were making great progress. If my eyes weren't playing tricks on me, this path would eventually lead us by a more direct route back to the parking lot. I didn't look back as someone called out my name in a gruff tone. Was he still on the summit, or had he followed us using the same escape route we'd chosen? Could we beat him to the car? If not, then what?

2

Of Trails and Trials

"She was truest to them in the season of trial, as all the quietly loyal and good will always be."
—A Tale of Two Cities

∞

"FROM DEAD GHOSTS to old graves," Marty said. "What is it about the friends we keep?"

"Friends or not, the people who come to us for help are always going to do it because they're deeply troubled by a problem they can't solve on their own. Otherwise, why bother to hire the Grand Old Lady Detectives? For our friends, it's also a chance for us to be 'truest to them in their season of trial,'" Charly replied.

"Nicely put! The line about a 'season of trial' is from *A Tale of Two Cities*, isn't it?" Neely asked. The phrase sounded familiar to me, but I could never have made the connection as Neely quickly had. "Inspired, no doubt, by the fact that your friend, Judith Rogow, is convinced the grave she wants us to find is on Dickens' Dune."

"Don't look at me," Joe said as my eyes settled on him for a split second. He was piling food on his plate from a sidebar where Midge had set up our potluck buffet style. As usual, when my friends and I get together, we eat. There's comfort in food, especially when the topic is foul play, now that our "active adult" pursuits include sleuthing. That was especially true for me, given my unexpected "trial" on the trail this morning.

"I've never read *A Tale of Two Cities*. The only Dickens story I know is the one about Scrooge. That one was about ghosts *and* graves. Marley was some ghost, too!" Carl nodded in agreement with Joe's commentary on Dickens' *A Christmas Carol*. That story had made Scrooge a holiday icon almost as well-known as Santa.

"He had heavy-duty chains to rattle, that's for sure," Carl added. The two men, who are best buddies and fancy themselves to be "Charly's Angels," high-fived each other. "Whether in the best of times or worst of times, Dickens' writing is often preoccupied with the dark side."

"Well, he didn't shirk from looking square in the face at the problems of his day, if that's what you mean. He was a radical with a critical eye, although Scrooge ended up as a transformed man. Pip, in *Great Expectations*, did too. Still, he can be gloomy. Maybe that's appropriate since we have a sad, old murder on our hands. I hope we can do more than offer support to your friend, Charly. Her 'season of trial' would end better with her ex-husband's killer on trial in a courtroom," Midge offered, sighing as she spoke.

As an avowed Anglophile, who lives in the Austen Cottage, Midge's comment about Charles Dickens being gloomy was a little surprising. Perhaps her disposition was due more to the case than the author for whom Dickens'

Dune had been named. Midge bit into a slice of Amish Tomato Pie, her eyes rolled heavenward, and her mood changed instantly.

The pie recipe is a favorite from my old life in Ohio before my husband's sudden death sent me west to Seaview Cottages. References to renowned writers like Dickens are everywhere in this area. That's especially true in the Writers' Circle where we all reside in cottages bearing authors' names.

"We don't know yet that Leonard Cohen's deathbed confession is true. If it is, and Judith's ex-husband is dead and buried on Dickens' Dune, I don't want to raise her expectation that our investigation will bring his killer to justice. Who knows if the killer is even alive?" Charly asked and sent a sideways glance my way.

Had Neely caught that? I wondered as Neely pursed her lips and her brow furrowed.

When I got home from Dickens' Dune this morning, I called Charly and explained what had happened. In the safety and comfort of my Hemingway Cottage, it all seemed less dire than it had when Domino and I had run for it. Charly told me then what she was telling everyone else now—that Allen Rogow's killer was most likely dead.

She repeated what I'd already told myself. We hadn't been involved in the investigation of Allen Rogow's disappearance long enough to have stirred up much interest in tailing me or anyone else. She'd also pointed out that murderous cutthroats usually work alone and don't bring a laughing woman along with them when they're stalking their next victim.

"It is an odd coincidence, and I don't like coincidences

that occur anywhere near an old murder scene, so cool it, okay?" She'd added.

"I've learned my lesson. No lone wolf behavior when we're working on a murder case. You've already told us that, but it's a cold case, so I didn't even think about it until Domino and I got out there on the trail."

"Trust your instincts, Miriam. The minute you feel uncomfortable, change course, especially when you're in an isolated setting like that. Let me see if I can get someone to help us identify the driver of the car parked next to the guy wielding those binoculars. That plate looks like one used by a rental car company."

Fortunately, even in my frantic flight, I'd had the presence of mind to pull out my cellphone. I'd snapped a couple of photos of the license plate on the car parked in the lot before taking off. I tried to let it go and refocus on what Charly was saying now.

"I believe Judith would settle for knowing where her ex-husband's body is buried and, perhaps, moving him to consecrated ground," Charly added as she addressed all of us.

"That's good to hear, but how are we going to find his body decades later when the police weren't able to do it while the trail was still warm?" Marty asked with an anxious expression on her face.

I'd asked myself the same question many times in the few days we'd spent recovering from the startling revelations behind a series of unfortunate events at Shakespeare Cottage. The property is still under armed guard, as federal agents work with local and state police to recover pricy stolen property and search for clues about the owners' involvement in a smuggling ring. The crime lab had already collected evidence about two murders from the location. Who knows what other secrets remain for the authorities to find? I flashed on the image of the man with those binoculars.

Does he have an ax to grind about my involvement in that mess? I wondered before I responded to Marty's question.

"We didn't have much to go on when we began looking into Robyn's troubles in the Shakespeare Cottage, so who knows what we'll dig up."

"Yuck, yuck," Neely interjected. "Pun intended I assume. When it comes to digging up old bones, let's leave it to the dogs."

"No one on two legs or four legs is going to disturb Allen Rogow's resting place if we find it. Not until the crime lab folks have had a crack at it," Charly interjected in a firm voice. "You can do all the digging you want in cyberspace, but no poking around on the dune until we have a better understanding of what we've taken on by agreeing to help Judith." Charly caught my eye once again, and I nodded. This time, I was sure Neely noticed the brief exchange before she spoke.

"I've already read the old news I could find about Allen Rogow's disappearance, which isn't much. Social media didn't exist; no Facebook or Twitter or Instagram. The Internet wasn't used by us regular folk much then either. I can try to do a search of online newspaper archives. We might find useful information if the story of Allen Rogow's disappearance got picked up by the national news outlets."

"I already tried to do that, Neely, but without any luck. I think we need to make a trip to Duneville Down Public Library and go through their microfiche archives the old-fashioned way. What we do have that the police didn't have when Judith Rogow's ex-husband went missing, is Leonard Cohen and his deathbed confession about Allen Rogow's murder. That's a fresh place to start."

"Won't the police do that and look into the matter again now that they have Leonard Cohen's confession?" Marty asked.

"That's a very good question. It's the first issue that concerned me once Judith explained why she wanted to hire us. Judith's convinced that no one cared much about Allen's disappearance at the time even though there were suspicious circumstances. She felt they saw him as just one more troubled vet who'd turned to drugs to solve his problems, and she doesn't believe they'll care more about it now. Since I spoke to her, I've used my contacts with the local police to see if there's a cold case team, or anyone else assigned to take a new look at Allen Rogow's case. So far, Judith appears to be right that no one's chomping at the bit to do anything."

"At least we won't be stepping on anyone's toes," Joe pointed out. "I'm not looking forward to bumping into Deputy Devers again soon. He may not be as scary as the bad guys we've run into, but he's far more annoying."

"If you think he's been disagreeable in the past, wait until he finds out the insurance companies are paying us a reward for helping them recover millions of dollars in stolen art," Neely asserted.

"I'm not going to mention it, are you?" Marty asked. "Not unless he hears about it elsewhere and decides to go after Miriam. I'll have plenty to say to him if he annoys her after she made sure the insurance companies shared the reward with all of us."

"I would have given anything to see what was in that vault," Joe added. His eyes still bore the glint of what Detective Eddie Vargas had called "treasure hunt fever."

"Does that include your share of the reward?" Carl asked. That brought Joe to his senses.

"No, it does not. I'll settle for pictures taken by the evidence specialists, thank you very much," he replied. "If we ever get to see them."

"To be honest, I would have enjoyed being the one to open the vault," I said. "The reward money is a great consolation prize, and I have no doubt that Charly can find someone who will share the photos with us."

Consolation prize is an understatement. The money was a godsend given how close to the edge of financial disaster I've lived since I became a widow and inherited a legacy of debt my husband had skillfully hidden. He'd depleted our savings, and the pension I receive as his widow is barely enough to live month-to-month. Thanks to the windfall coming from the insurance companies, I felt like I could breathe again for the first time since Pete died more than a year ago.

"The next time you and Hank go out for dinner, why not work it into the conversation? Maybe you can arrange a trade—cookies or one of these delicious tomato pies in exchange for pics!" Neely teased.

I wanted to come up with a witty retort, but I'm still

tongue-tied at the mention of my personal involvement with the detective. That's especially true now that, at fifty, he'd been my first date in three decades. Charly came to my rescue.

"He's already promised to share the pictures with us," Charly responded. "Let's save the food as a bribery option until we need it again. So far, it has come in handy, but I don't want to push our luck."

"Miriam's treats have been helpful as a way to put people at ease and start a conversation, that's for sure," Neely said. "More like an ice breaker than a bribe."

"Which we don't need with Hank. Not only has Miriam broken the ice but from what I've heard they're going public with their relationship. She's his date for the County Sheriff's barbeque fundraiser." Charly winked as everyone stared at me.

My mouth fell open since I hadn't told her about it. Nor had I used the word "date" when I referred to the lovely evening that Hank and I had shared over dinner. I prefer to think of my "relationship" with Hank as the start of a friendship, not a romance. Still, Hank had called it a date when he asked me to go with him to the fundraiser. Had he mentioned it to Charly, or were the local gossips whispering about it?

"I'm sure Hank told you it's, uh, for a good cause," I stammered. "They're raising money for their K-9 Unit. He also must have told you that he doesn't like going to those events alone." Charly didn't give anything away. Joe smirked as I squirmed until, mercifully, Carl switched the subject and placed Joe's love life center stage.

"Joe's already been on his second date with Robyn,

right, Romeo?"

"Yep! Robyn is a better golfer than you are. Better than me, too, but I don't mind a challenge, do you?" Joe asked, probably hoping Carl would jump into the fray and set off a round of banter. When Carl merely shrugged, Joe gave up. "Can we get back to business since now that you brought it up, I promised to go look at a golf cart with Robyn later this afternoon? If it's in good enough shape, she's going to buy it and move it into her garage when the sale closes on her cottage."

"We don't have much more business to discuss until Judith Rogow joins us for dessert. I hope she can give us more background about her ex-husband's disappearance. Memory is an odd thing—it fades over time, but sometimes when revisiting the past, a new piece of information works its way into the retelling of the story," Midge suggested.

"I hope you're right," I said as I finished the salad that Midge had made to go with our pie. It was her turn to host a gathering of our group. The Austen Cottage reflected Midge's love of old English country cottage décor, but she'd artfully blended it with her practical, no-frills approach to life.

The chair in which I sat, in the sunroom Midge had added to the cottage, was part of a pair of high-backed armchairs upholstered in a gold toile. Two loveseats arranged in an L-shape, opposite the armchairs, sported a solid color in a deeper gold. Botanicals, plaids, and stripes were used in throw pillows, but there were no precious fabrics and not nearly as much lace and florals as were evident in Charly's Brontë Cottage. Like all the other cottages in our circle, including my own, books were everywhere.

In addition to the glorious sunroom in which we sat, I envied two things about Midge's cottage. The first was an amazing stone fireplace in the great room that was original to the cottage when it was built in the sixties. The second was Midge's enchanting garden, which sprawled out before us with a view of the golf course beyond.

"I had no idea Midge had such a green thumb," I'd exclaimed when I first stepped into the conservatory, with its high, angled glass roof a few weeks ago.

"Why wouldn't she?" Neely had asked. "Midge has dedicated her life to the healing arts. Don't let her brusqueness fool you, she's skilled at nurturing and restoring what's good in the world around her." Neely's words were easy to believe. Although Midge currently had no canine companion, she had no qualms about having us bring our dogs to her home.

Domino and Charly's spunky Jack Russell Terrier, Emily, were loose in the backyard. They were both being very well behaved, lying in the shade produced by an arbor covered in purple blooms. The garden was a stunning testament to Midge's command of the ground on which her two feet were so firmly placed. It also revealed a more poetic side that explained Midge's devotion to English literature, and a fleeting flirtation with the theater when she was younger. Charly spoke, and the tone in her voice abruptly ended my contemplation of Midge's garden and the golf course beyond.

"I said we don't have much more business to take care of before Judith arrives, but I do have one more issue we need to get out in the open."

"Don't keep us in suspense. Tell us, please, Charly!" Marty exclaimed.

3

Heavenly Compassion

"Dead, men and women, born with Heavenly compassion in your hearts. And dying thus around us every day."

—Bleak House

∞

"YES, TELL US, please! I am so relieved. I was afraid I was going to have to rough up you two before you told us what was going on with all the sidelong glances and a warning to stay away from Dickens' Dune. What's up?"

"That isn't what I was going to say next. If you insist, I'll let Miriam give you a quick rundown on an incident at Dickens' Dune this morning. I'm not convinced it has anything to do with the disappearance of Judith's ex-husband, or I would already have asked Miriam to share her experience with us."

"Charly is being kind. What she means is that she's trying to keep me from embarrassing myself, given my unprovoked panic this morning," I sighed deeply and then rushed through a brief account of what had gone on. I included what I'd seen when I stopped at the bunker and how that related to the history I'd found online.

As I retold the story, it seemed even more ludicrous for me to have run like a scared rabbit. Dangerous, too. At one point, when I'd peeked over my shoulder to see if the guy was barreling down the hillside after us, a snake had slithered across the unkempt trail.

"Are you sure you've seen him before?" Carl asked.

"I think so, but I must be wrong since I can't say where. If Charly can get a name by checking on the license plate, maybe that'll jog my memory. In the meantime, she's asked the security guards at the gate to notify us if anyone driving that car asks for access to the golf course or wants to dine at the clubhouse."

"Well, your description of that bunker is disturbing enough to give me the willies long distance," Marty added, rubbing her arms as if she'd felt a sudden chill. "It's a murder den if I ever heard of one!"

"I agree. Surely, the police would have examined the place, thoroughly, if Allen Rogow was attacked anywhere near there," Neely responded, with her voice rising as if her comment was actually a question.

"I can tell you more once I get a copy of whatever police reports are still around. As we learned when we investigated Cookie DeVoss's disappearance in the early seventies, the County Sheriff's Department and Forensics weren't anything like they are today. Even a decade later, when Allen went missing, the department wasn't equipped to collect evidence as well as it is today. If the incidents had occurred more recently, I'd already have the police reports, but it's a cold case that was opened before the information was stored electronically. The files are probably in boxes on a shelf somewhere."

"There must be a few people around who remember the incident. Public access to that old bunker was closed off not long after he vanished. Whatever happened there, must have had something to do with the decision to close it. If that's the case, we might be able to find someone who remembers details about what happened and how that figured into the decision to place the bunker off limits," I suggested.

"As unappealing as the location seems to be to us, Allen might have considered it a refuge," Midge suggested. "Homeless Vietnam vets often felt safer hidden away in a place like that."

"As far as outdoor sanctuaries go, the old bunker seems to have seen more traffic than most," Neely commented.

"Allen wasn't a recluse if he wasn't just using drugs, but also dealing them," Carl added, "he might have chosen that spot as a place to do business without being observed by the authorities."

"That's very perceptive, Carl. It brings me back to what I wanted to say to you. If Judith brings it up, fine. If not, you'll have the information as context for whatever she does share with us." Charly's words hung in the air as I picked up the fine cup of Darjeeling tea Midge had prepared.

"I'm not sure it's mentioned in the articles you found about Allen's disappearance, but there's a reason an ex-convict knows so much about him. He was among the last of the U.S. troops to leave Vietnam. According to Judith, Allen was a changed man when he returned to California from Vietnam near the end of 1974."

"Hold on," Carl interrupted. "The last troops left in 1973 after the fall of Saigon. Why didn't Allen Rogow return to California until a year later? Was he a POW?"

"You're right about the troop withdrawal," Charly replied and was instantly cut off by Joe.

"Wow, you're firing on all cylinders today, amigo! Why didn't I think of that?" There was a pause that ended when Neely snorted.

"You don't really want any of us to come up with witty retorts to that question, do you?" Joe shrugged, made eye contact with Neely, and then shook his head no. Charly continued.

"Judith expected Allen to return home in 1973," Charly replied. "When he didn't show up, she began trying to track him down. She finally got a cryptic letter from him. He wasn't a POW. He was in a German hospital being treated for gunshot wounds that had nearly killed him. Judith says she couldn't get a straight answer from him or anyone else about how the shooting had occurred or why she wasn't notified that he'd been wounded. When he arrived back in the states, Allen explained that he'd also been hospitalized for mental health problems. Probably post-traumatic stress disorder, although he didn't call it that, and she wasn't sure what diagnosis he was given."

"I can guess at what she meant when she said Allen was a changed man. My cousin returned to Ohio in bad shape. He struggled most of his life after that," I said. "It must have been hard for her."

"It *was* hard, which is another reason I'm not sure how

much detail she'll want to go into today. Her distress was obvious as she explained it to me. They had young children at home, and Allen wasn't only unstable but, on occasion, he would erupt in angry outbursts. What she didn't know right away was that he'd developed a dependency on pain killers."

"As a result of his treatment for the gunshot wounds or was he using drugs before he was injured?" Midge asked.

"Allen told her he was given pain medication in the hospital and tried to kick it but couldn't do it. A bullet had permanently damaged his knee and, apparently, the pain never went away. She's not sure if his drug use was strictly because of the knee injury, though. When she confronted him about his drug use, it was because she'd stumbled across a stash of marijuana as well as all sorts of pills."

"If you're right about PTSD, he wouldn't have been the first vet to self-medicate in an attempt to deal with his troubled mind as well as his physical pain," Midge added. "Carl's point about dealing rather than just using drugs, is a good one since that's one of the ways some addicts support their habit."

"That's a good guess about what was going on. Allen was arrested and spent two years in the state prison for drug possession and dealing."

"To get a two-year sentence in prison rather than probation or jail time, must mean that wasn't his first offense or they caught him with lots of pills," Midge added.

"I came to the same conclusion. Judith said she wasn't aware of any earlier arrests, but who knows? Maybe a buddy bailed him out, and he kept the incident from her. I've asked for his arrest records, too. If I can get them, I'll be able to give you more details," Charly assured us.

"Now I get it! That's what you meant when you said you could explain how an ex-convict knows so much about Allen and his secrets!" Joe exclaimed.

"It does. I urged Judith to meet with us and share whatever she feels is important for us to know. I assume that will include some disclosure about Allen's drug problems and the time he spent in prison. If not, I'll bring it up. Our meeting is more about being supportive and building trust rather than grilling a witness or a suspect in a crime." Charly looked at each of us, and then stopped and fixed her gaze on Joe and Carl.

"Okay, so no 'bad cop' today." Carl elbowed Joe and shook his head no.

"No 'cop' at all!" Charly added. "We want to display compassion—'Heavenly compassion'—to steal a couple of words from Charles Dickens."

"I got it. Compassion is my middle name," Joe replied and turned toward Carl. "You'd better keep those boney elbows to yourself if you want her to trust us."

"Trust must be difficult for Judith after all she's gone through," I said.

"Yes. Her ex-husband's secrecy got to Judith at least as much as the problems he revealed to her. She quit trusting him."

"Who could blame her? With young children to protect, she didn't just have her own safety to consider. It must have become more than she could bear. I assume she divorced him and that's why you refer to him as her ex-husband," I suggested.

"Allen was the one who initiated divorce proceedings, not Judith, shortly after he was released from prison. It wasn't too long after the divorce was finalized that he disappeared. When you hear her talk about it, you'll be able to tell how much she's still longing for closure. Judith was haunted by the possibility that he'd committed suicide and blamed herself for agreeing to the divorce."

"It can't be any more pleasant to learn that he was murdered, but maybe it'll put an end to that old guilt," Marty commented.

"How awful to have him return from Vietnam, and lose him again to prison, divorce, and then have him vanish altogether. I don't want to ask if you already have an answer for us, Charly. Did the police ever consider Judith as a suspect in his disappearance?" I asked.

"An ex-wife is always on the list," Charly replied. "Judith claims she'd taken the children to Anaheim for a vacation to Disneyland. He visited the children before they left for Anaheim, and that was the last time she and the children ever saw him. I assume the police checked out her story right away. That would have given her a solid alibi." For some reason, I felt relieved to hear that, even though from what Charly told us about Judith, it was hard to imagine her as a killer.

"I hope she hasn't spent her entire life ruminating about his disappearance and deceitfulness," I said, in part chiding myself about how much time I still spend trying to fathom my husband's secret life.

"Judith is a strong woman who understands life is hard. She eventually remarried. No matter how it felt at the time, I bet Allen Rogow regarded divorce as an act of 'Heavenly compassion.' It took her a while to come to grips with the fact that the man she married returned so badly broken by whatever role he'd played during the war." I sensed something more in what Charly had just said. I wasn't the only one.

"By 'whatever role he played,' I take it he wasn't an ordinary Army Private First Class as his obit claimed," Neely said. Charly hesitated to respond.

"I'm not sure yet. Allen Rogow never trained for or became a member of Special Forces, so that's not the issue." Midge spoke up when Charly paused.

"If Allen Rogow was involved in Special Operations of some kind, that wouldn't necessarily be in his public record," Midge responded. "What is it they're not telling, or you're not telling us, Charly?"

"He doesn't appear to have had any special training or specific skills that might have earned him a Special Duty Assignment. However, Judith claims he received Special Duty Assignment pay for over a year before the end of the war."

"Does that have anything to do with Leonard Cohen's claim that Allen took secrets he'd promised to keep with him to his grave?" Carl asked.

"It could be. Sorting that out is only one challenge for our investigation. Judith was certain his Special Duty Assignment had something to do with his injuries and the mental anguish that tormented him. I'm doing what I can to find out more through ties I have outside the criminal justice system." Charly shrugged as I pondered what secrets her past held.

"If Leonard Cohen wasn't the only person who knew Allen's secrets, given how unstable he had become, someone could have decided to shut him up before he could give them up," Marty suggested.

"His secrets didn't have to be about Vietnam. Dealing drugs comes with the need to keep plenty of secrets," Joe said. "For all we know, a buyer or a supplier killed Allen when a drug deal went bad."

"It's too bad Judith wasn't in the room when Leonard Cohen made that confession," Neely added. "Did he say why he didn't come forward sooner?"

"Judith would have asked lots of good questions like that, including who told him Allen was murdered and where he was buried," Marty huffed. "Surely, she quizzed the nurse to whom Leonard Cohen made his confession and asked her questions like that."

"We need to speak to his nurse regardless of what questions Judith or the police have asked her—if they've bothered to follow up," Midge asserted. Charly nodded in agreement.

"That's a good idea. Before she leaves today, let's make sure Judith gives us the nurse's name," Charly said, making a note for herself.

"I'd like to know more about Leonard Cohen. Who was he? What do we know about him and why he was sent to prison?" I asked. "What if his nurse wasn't the only person with whom he shared his regrets? Did he have any close associates or friends who visited him? How about a wife or some other family member?"

"I haven't asked Judith any of those questions. All she told me was that Leonard was adamant that his nurse contact Judith and let her know what had happened to her ex-husband, that Allen loved her, and none of his troubles were her fault."

"That must mean he and Allen were close," I commented. "Are you sure they met in prison?"

"Once she understands how eager we are to help, I can't believe she won't at least bring up the fact that he and Allen were inmates at the same time. Given the secret life Allen led, she may not know how they met, but let's ask her."

As if on cue, the doorbell rang. Judith had arrived. Midge hurried toward the door with Charly at her side. We sat in silent anticipation. I stared out the window as a foursome of golfers stopped on the fairway, stepped from their carts, and walked to the tee. The public course draws a steady stream of guests now that the summer visitors have arrived. Usually, golfers at play made me happy. Today, though, I was uncomfortable about how easy it was for outsiders to gain access to our "gated community." Apparently, Midge's suspicions had gone in a different direction during our silence.

"Leonard Cohen's sudden gesture of 'Heavenly compassion' seems to be an odd way of making amends if that's truly what he was doing," Midge asserted.

"He could have hoped to get long-delayed justice for his murdered friend. Under the law, his deathbed confession could be introduced into court as new evidence. It's not regarded as hearsay," Carl pointed out.

"Confessing someone else's sins isn't exactly what I'd call a deathbed confession," Neely interjected. "He didn't say he killed Allen. In fact, we don't even know if the information he disclosed was based on firsthand knowledge of what happened to Allen." I wanted to hear the rest of what Neely had to say, but my phone rang.

I dug the phone out of my purse and answered it even though I didn't recognize the caller's phone number. The sudden windfalls that had improved my financial situation hadn't stopped me from searching for a bookkeeping job. Maybe someone was following up on one of the applications I'd left around town.

"Hello," I said.

"Miriam Webster, please."

"This is she," I responded. Click! The call ended. I held out the phone and looked at the caller's number.

"What is it?" Neely asked, apparently reading the confusion on my face. "A wrong number?"

My mind raced down several paths at once, trying to figure out how best to answer Neely's question. It couldn't be a wrong number since the caller had asked for me by name. Was the man's voice vaguely familiar or was my imagination running wild again?

4

A Better Shape

"I have been bent and broken, but – I hope – into a better shape."

—Great Expectations

∞

"IT WASN'T A wrong number. The caller asked for me by name and then hung up."

"That's weird," Marty said, her brow wrinkled. "All you need is more weirdness after your experience this morning. Was it a man?" I nodded, yes.

"The same man who spoke to you at Dickens' Dune?" Neely asked.

"Maybe." Then I shook my head. "I don't know—that guy hollered my name—this one was speaking barely above a whisper. It was kind of creepy, now that you ask."

"As in heavy breathing creepy?" Joe asked.

"Obscene callers don't usually ask for you by name," Marty observed.

"It's more likely to be a telemarketer. They use random digit dialing until they find a number that belongs to a real person, then you get a dozen calls trying to sell you a vacation cruise or window replacement. Is your mobile number on a 'do not call' list?"

"No," I replied, although I was deep in thought. Carl's idea about the telemarketing routine didn't explain how the caller already knew my name.

"Give me the phone," Neely demanded. Before I could ask her why, she'd taken the phone and redialed the number. "It didn't go through. Carl must be right."

"Block it. That'll slow down the barrage of calls to come," Carl suggested.

"That's a great idea." At least, whoever had called wouldn't be able to do it again without making a little extra effort. It took me a few seconds to figure out how to block the call. I wished that I'd gotten a closer look at the man I'd seen on Dickens' Dune this morning. That might have made it easier to recall where I'd seen him before and determine if his face matched the voice of the man who had just called me on the phone.

Carl could still be right that the call originated with a telemarketing firm. Not a random call as he suggested, but one targeted to my name and number. Then why hang up? Why not make his pitch?

When Charly and Midge stepped back into the sunroom, I put aside my worries about the phone call. Instead, I focused on the imposing figure of a woman who entered the room with them. Judith Rogow was taller than both Midge and Charly. I judged her to be in her seventies, but I might have guessed she was younger if I hadn't already known as much as I did about her background.

The well-dressed woman wore her dark hair pulled

back into a bun. Her business suit fit perfectly, and I suddenly felt woefully underdressed. Marty was the only one among us who could pass off her outfit as "business casual." Charly, whose empathic ability must have been set on "high," introduced us and instantly put us at ease.

"Judith Rogow, I'd like you to meet the rest of the G.O.L.D. team including those two," Charly said as she pointed at Joe and Carl. Then she introduced each of us by name. "Please don't apologize again for showing up in business attire. We're happy you were able to squeeze in a visit with us on a day when you have important obligations to your charity work."

"I'm glad to meet all the women of G.O.L.D. and Charly's Angels." Carl and Joe smiled.

"At your service," Carl said in a snappy tone. "I wish we were meeting under more auspicious circumstances, but we're happy to help."

"I'm glad to find you none the worse for wear after your harrowing experience in Shakespeare Cottage. In fact, I was amazed at how composed you all seemed to be in the video captured by the local television news team as you left the cottage. You must be getting lots of requests for assistance now that your exploits as sleuths have become newsworthy."

"We don't quite have our act together. There's no easy way for members of the public to track us down. I have had several referrals passed along from the Sheriff's PR department and the local TV station," Charly said as Midge steered Judith to one of the big, comfy armchairs in the room.

"I'll be right back with dessert and tea," Midge said.

"Charly's correct that we haven't figured out how to advertise our services, but there's something to be said for 'word of mouth' referrals. In fact, I almost prefer it that way."

"So far, the requests that have come in are for what Charly tells us is the 'bread and butter' of private detective work—background checks on people new to their business or social circles, concerns about a cheating spouse or two-timing paramour, and in the case of a local small business owner, a request for personal injury surveillance after an employee filed for workers' compensation," Marty commented.

"We've already got that one figured out," Joe said. "Carl and I jumped on the surveillance work and got to the bottom of the workers' comp fraud caper."

"With backup from Miriam and me. Once they spotted the guy talking up a storm with some woman at a dog park, Miriam and I showed up with Domino," Marty said, pointing to my sweet Dalmatian. She and her pal, Emily, were at the back door, peering in to check out our visitor. They must have approved since they were both wearing big doggie grins and furiously wagging their tails. I would have let them in except that I was sure they'd get dog hairs all over the lovely tailored suit Judith wore. As Carl picked up where Marty had left off, I got up, went to the door, and tossed a treat to each of them.

"The guy was unbelievable!" Carl exclaimed. "Two minutes after they started chatting him up, he was cavorting with Domino. His back was in better shape than mine."

"Which isn't saying much. You creak and squeak like

an old door that needs oiling with WD-40," Joe quipped. "We got the action on video, though, and quickly closed that case."

"Except for surveillance, most of the routine work can be done without leaving our cottages. Have laptop! Will snoop!" Then Neely snapped her fingers.

"You know what, Miriam? Judith may have just solved the riddle of the new man in your life. Maybe it's some guy who saw you on TV and wants to ask for our help, but he's nervous about it." Neely didn't go into detail but briefly explained to Judith that I'd had two odd incidents in one day involving a strange man.

"I can understand it if he's nervous. It's not easy to ask for help from strangers," Judith responded. "I was so relieved when someone at the Temple Sinai Community Center mentioned how helpful Charly had been to Edgar Humphrey when his son got into trouble. Having a friend to ask for help makes it a little easier."

"We'll do everything we can to merit your trust and find out whatever we can about what happened to your ex-husband." I was about to sit back down when Midge came into the room carrying a tray laden with the sour cream coffee cake I'd brought for dessert and a fresh pot of tea. I took the teapot from the tray, savoring the hint of lemon cast off by the steamy tea. Midge set the coffee cake on the sidebar near a stack of vintage bone china dessert plates with beautiful botanical prints on them. While Midge cut the cake, I poured a cup of tea for Judith and then sorted out who else wanted another cup.

"Charly has shared your story with us, but we'd like to hear it from you if you're willing to tell it again," I said after she'd had a sip of tea. "We're curious to learn what you know about Leonard Cohen, although Charly's already conducting a formal background check on him." Judith smiled as she set her cup in its saucer, picked up her cake, and replied to my comment.

"Well, I might be able to do a better job retelling the story now that the initial shock has worn off a little. It won't take long to tell you all I know about Leonard Cohen. I first met him decades ago when we were children in Santa Maria. He and his family went to the same synagogue that my family and I attended. We were in grade school together, too. He was a skinny, annoying little boy with enormous glasses. A year younger than me, he followed me around."

"A crush, huh?" Carl asked.

"It could be. He got bullied a lot, so I stuck up for him now and then. As far as I can recall, he was the only other Jewish kid at school. That wasn't the main reason he was picked on, but it ticked me off when someone brought religion into it. I was tall for my age, and I had a mouth on me even then with a voice that carried. It's a good thing I didn't have your kubotan, Charly. I might have been tempted to use it to give the school bullies more than a tongue-lashing." Judith paused to eat a bite of the coffee cake. I held my breath. For some reason, it had suddenly become important to me that she liked it. She did.

"Miriam, this is delicious. I'd love to have your recipe if you'll share it."

"Of course, I'll share it. I'm glad you like it. It's one of dozens of recipes I rescued when the bakery I worked for went out of business. They were excellent bakers, but not very good managers. I tried to get them to raise the price on their products with no luck." I stopped speaking since I was babbling about an irrelevant topic. Judith didn't seem to mind as she ate more of the cake. Everyone else was eating, too, amid a chorus of oohs and ahs.

"Miriam ought to start a sideline. 'G.O.L.D.'s Bakery—where to find the best baked goods is no mystery!'" Neely exclaimed using the back of her hand to give her glasses a shove. "I'll be a willing taste tester to ensure the quality is always first rate."

"Angel deliveries are on us. We'll work for cookie dough, won't we, Carl?" Carl was up on his feet heading to the sidebar for a second piece of cake.

"You won't get an argument from me!" He said and then paused to ask Judith a question. "Did you know your old friend had ended up in prison?"

"No. We lost touch by the time we went to middle school. By then, he'd distinguished himself academically, so I figured he was on his way to great things. I was as shocked to discover that Leonard was in prison as I was when Allen ended up there." She glanced around at us. "I'm sure that Charly already explained that's how Allen and Leonard became acquainted."

"We weren't sure how they met since she didn't give us much detail," I said. "I suppose Allen told Leonard that you were his wife, and that's how he knew to get a message to you."

"Yes. While they were both confined to The Men's Colony just north of San Luis Obispo, Leonard and Allen spoke frequently. They were in AA meetings together, although Allen's problems involved more than alcohol abuse. Leonard was in prison for financial fraud involving a Ponzi scheme or a phony fund of some kind that went belly up. He was a smalltime Bernie Madoff before anyone had ever heard of that rat. Even though he'd used his talents to become a crook, I was grateful for Leonard's kindness toward Allen. When I visited Allen, I brought care packages that always included a few goodies for Leonard." She polished off her cake and set the plate on the table next to her.

"Nothing with a file baked into it, I guess." Joe snickered.

"Will you stop? He promised to be on his best behavior today. Charly's Angels sometimes fancy themselves to be throwbacks to Lewis and Martin."

"Hey, we're good at coming up with clues, but we're not great explorers like those guys," Joe smirked. Carl snorted, and Neely rolled her eyes.

"He knows I didn't mean Lewis and Clark," Neely muttered. "Some guys remain annoying little boys all their lives."

"Well, it was Martin and Lewis—not Lewis and Martin. You confused my old pal," Carl said. Joe nodded his head vigorously in agreement. Neely harrumphed.

"Charly told me 'angels' might be a misnomer," Judith smiled when Joe's mouth popped open. "No, Joe. I never took them cakes filled with anything other than massive amounts of hope. They were fortunate to have been imprisoned in a place that had support for inmates with alcohol and drug problems. I wanted them to come out of there clean and sober and with a fresh start on life." Judith stared into her teacup without saying another word for a minute before she looked up. "I kept hoping for the day when Allen would tell me he'd been bent and broken, but into a better shape."

"I love that line. It could have come from the pen of Charlotte Brontë instead of Dickens," Charly sighed. Judith's sorrow bore down on us like a cloud. A big, fat dark one. It would have been heavy enough to smother hope altogether in someone less resilient than Judith Rogow must have been.

"I'm sorry that didn't happen," I said.

"I am too. Not everyone can transcend suffering or come through it in better shape," Judith responded as she met my gaze and held it. Had Charly told her about my own poor ill-fated marriage to a man who got in over his head without giving me a clue he was in trouble? "To be honest, I was pretty worn out with Allen, but I would have gone another round when he was released from prison if he'd been willing to do it. Instead, he filed for divorce, moved out, and then vanished a few months later."

"Moved out?" Neely asked. "Where? Was he living alone or with someone else?" Before she could answer that question, out of the corner of my eye, a golf cart sped by. It wasn't on the greens, but on the cart path that ran between Midge's backyard and the golf course. That wasn't an unusual sight, but the loud "pop" that followed had us all on our feet.

"Down!" Charly shouted and we all ducked for cover.

5

A Heart that Never Hardens

"Have a heart that never hardens and a temper that never tires, and a touch that never hurts."

—Hard Times

∞

"IT'S OKAY!" MIDGE said in a firm, confident tone. "We're not under attack! That's the sound of a golf ball hitting the side of my cottage. It's the price I pay for living this close to the tee-box."

"Are you sure?" Marty asked as we reclaimed our seats. It would take a little longer for my jangled nerves to settle down.

"Yes, I'm sure. It's a monthly occurrence this time of the year. I should have warned you, but it happens so rarely I don't think about it until I take a hit or I'm bringing in someone to fix the dings left on the side of my house."

"You're a brave woman to have added a glass room onto the back of the house," Judith remarked in a light-hearted way.

"That stand of trees deflects the golf balls that could

hit us here. Most drivers off the tee slice right at an angle that misses me, but occasionally, I get hit like today. I'm sorry we were distracted from a far more important matter. You were going to tell us where Allen lived after he was released from prison."

"Oh, yes. Initially, Allen was released to a halfway house. It was a sober living residence, which I considered to be a good thing. He was supposed to return home after that, but filed for divorce instead, and left the halfway house without even giving me a forwarding address. I begged for information about him, still hoping I could change his mind about the divorce. One of the residents of the halfway house finally took pity on me and slipped me a note with an address on it." She stopped speaking as if trying to compose herself and didn't look at any of us as she continued. "When I went to that address, a woman answered the door. She was obviously loaded and maybe high on something too. I asked to speak to Allen, and she told me he didn't want to see me. She also insisted I go away and change my name because there was a new Mrs. Rogow in his future."

"No!" I gasped, silently thankful that Pete had spared me that humiliation. That's presuming I'd unraveled all his secrets. *Had there been other women in his life?* I wondered as I struggled to speak. "What did you say to her?"

"What could I say? I left, but I didn't really believe her. Eventually, Allen contacted me again to make visitation arrangements to see the children. He assured me she was a housemate with an all-too-vivid imagination. I figured that was an attempt to avoid the obvious issue that they'd met through rehab or a support group, and she was a drug user."

"Did you try to change his mind about the divorce?" Neely asked.

"Yes, but he was determined, and I was too tired by that point to fight him anymore. I didn't change my name, though. While Allen was in Vietnam, I'd educated myself as an accountant. By the time he got out of prison, I had finally managed to establish myself, professionally, as Judith Rogow. Even if I wanted to do it, I was known in San Luis Obispo by that name and didn't want to lose ground by changing it."

"Did you get the name of the woman you spoke to?" Neely asked.

"I heard someone inside the apartment call her Wendy. Wendy Ballard was the name on the mailbox when I checked on my way out of the apartment building."

"Why didn't you believe her?" Marty asked.

"Call me a fool for love if you want to, but I was still convinced Allen meant what he said when he'd promised to love me forever. A promise he'd made publicly before family and friends when we exchanged marriage vows. Before God, too, since he was religious at the time. What I didn't fully understand, I guess, was that the Allen Rogow who made that vow never came back from Vietnam. Still, Leonard's message conveyed what I felt in my heart all along—that Allen hadn't stopped loving me."

"Charly told us how deeply affected Allen was by his experience in Vietnam—including the dependence he developed on pain medications after he was shot and nearly killed. Did Allen ever try to explain what had happened to him?" Carl asked.

"Nothing specific. When I pushed him to be more open with me, he listed all the miseries that I've since heard from other Vietnam vets. The list is a long one—the mud, mosquitos, heat, trying to avoid contact with chemicals, lousy food, and no sleep. The relentless gunfire, landmines, booby traps, and snares set up in the jungle, as well as attacks coming from civilians—even kids. Watching their comrades die. I know it's nothing that wasn't on the nightly news back then, but the distress was palpable in his eyes, and in the trembling of his voice and lips. I did my best to comfort him without knowing the whole story." Judith's voice broke. "I was so angry when I couldn't reach him, but I forgave him for everything when I saw how hard it still was for other vets even years later. It's all the things I still don't know that haunt me."

"I'm sorry he couldn't have been more forthcoming with you," Midge responded almost in a whisper. "Some vets find relief in sharing their ordeal, but not everyone does."

"I believe Allen found that hard to do because he had secrets he couldn't share. I don't know if those were secrets tied to a Special Duty Assignment that he had in Vietnam or something more personal that happened while he was there. A couple of times, he let things slip about the price you pay for trusting the wrong people. Once, he told me that not all the bad guys were on the other side." I glanced at Charly as she commented on what Judith had just said.

"I told them about the Special Duty Assignment Pay Allen received. I'm doing what I can to find out what he did to earn it, and if that's how he was wounded. I hope I can share what I learn with you now that it's been more than forty years since he was injured."

"I'd appreciate it. Thank you." Judith said, sighing. She lapsed into a somber silence.

"I know this has to be difficult for you. We'll do our best to fill in the gaps. Do you know what Allen was doing in this area when he vanished?" I asked, hoping to restart our conversation.

"I can't be sure. He and his family used to vacation here when he was a child. They rented one of the summer cottages. More than once, Allen said that he felt so free and happy here that it was as if he didn't have a care in the world. Before he began to withdraw and got arrested, we came here as a family once or twice. It seemed to boost his spirits, so maybe that's why he was here."

"From what you're saying, it makes perfect sense that he came here to sort things out," Charly suggested.

"It does, although he didn't have much money. I don't know how he got here or where he stayed. When the police found his dog tags and a few belongings on Dickens' Dune, they suggested he might have been camping on the beach."

"If he was here on a camping trip, what made them suspect foul play?" Marty asked.

"I'd filed a missing persons report when I tried to contact Allen about a family matter. Nick, a roommate who answered the phone, claimed he was no longer living there. Wendy was angry and evasive when I drove over to the apartment worried that Allen was still there but too sick or too drugged up to face me. She told me to get lost—that he'd gone home to live with his parents. I knew that wasn't true because the reason I called him in the first place was that he'd missed his Mom's birthday a few days earlier. When Wendy claimed he'd been gone for a week, I contacted the police. It was a couple of weeks later that hikers spotted those personal items, and called the police because there was blood on them."

"Was the blood a match to Allen's?"

"They didn't do DNA testing then, but the blood type was a match. They also found Allen's dog tags, and when they ran a check on them, they discovered the report I'd filed about his disappearance." She paused and gazed at us, making eye contact with Charly. "He wouldn't have given up those dog tags willingly, by the way. If he'd killed himself, he would have been wearing them." I wasn't as convinced as Judith was about that issue now that I knew how easily it was to be fooled by a man you believed you knew well. Then Joe made a very good point.

"He didn't bury himself," Joe said almost as if he was thinking aloud. Then he continued in a more empathetic tone. "Leonard had no reason to lie. I'm sure he was telling the truth when he said someone killed Allen. I just wish he'd told us who did it."

"I can make a guess," Marty added. "If Allen had come here to sort things out, it wouldn't surprise me if he was having second thoughts about his life. If that included his divorce, no matter what she said, Wendy Ballard may have thought he was going back to you. She wouldn't be the first scorned woman to seek revenge for being jilted."

"That would explain her evasiveness, and the fact that she was so angry with you, Judith," Midge added.

"If she was out of her mind on drugs at the time, it

would explain why she didn't take the dog tags with her or bury them with him. That would have made it harder to figure out Allen Rogow had ever been there," Carl suggested.

"Judith, could Allen have gotten involved with drugs again?" I asked.

"The police investigator asked me that once he'd looked into Allen's background. I told him I didn't know. Given my suspicions about Wendy Ballard's condition when I first met her, it wouldn't have surprised me. I suggested the police officer ask her that question. I must have sounded like a jealous ex-wife when I mentioned her because they took a closer look at me after that. They let go of the idea that I killed Allen once they found out the kids and I were in LA when Allen was on Dickens' Dune." Judith teared up at that point. Midge grabbed a tissue for her from a box sitting on a shelf.

"Thank you, Midge. I'm sorry. It was so frustrating to be treated as an overwrought ex-wife one minute, and as a murder suspect in the next."

"I get it, Judith. The police aren't always the most sensitive people, nor is their process always a logical one. I've asked for everything I can get from their archives about the investigation. Let us take it from there." She nodded as another question popped into my head.

"Who called out Wendy's name the first time you visited her?" I asked. "It wasn't Allen's voice, or you would have mentioned it. Could you tell if it was the same man you spoke to later—the roommate you called Nick?"

"I'm certain it was a different man. On my first visit, the man who spoke to Wendy sounded like one of Allen's

Army friends who hung out with him almost every week before Allen went to prison. He didn't bother coming to the door when she told him it was me, which didn't surprise me. Mark Viceroy wasn't a good influence on Allen. It wasn't just that he encouraged Allen to drink too much and do who knows what else, but Allen was always angry and more withdrawn after he'd visited. I heard them arguing more than once. Allen refused to tell me what the arguments were about or to cut off his buddies."

"Guys who served together forge strong bonds—like brothers," Midge offered.

"Yes. Allen's explanation was something like that. He wasn't going to cut off any of them because 'they've been through it all, too.' When I got the message from Leonard, one of the first things I did was try to track them down. I found obituaries for several of the men, but none for Mark Viceroy. The last I heard he was in prison."

"Maybe there's more information in the police record about Allen's friends and associates from interviews with his housemates. That was Allen's last known address; they should have spoken to everyone who lived there."

"There ought to be something in the case file about who they interviewed," Charly said.

"If they did interview them, it must have been a dead end since they never arrested Wendy or anyone else. In fact, the police told me that without a body, they couldn't even be certain that Allen was dead. One officer even suggested his disappearance was a message that he wanted to leave his past behind and that I should take the hint. I told them in no uncertain terms that if Allen was leaving the area, he would have said goodbye to his children, if not to me."

"Leonard Cohen has set that idea to rest," Charly assured her. Judith nodded and spoke to me.

"I did see Wendy Ballard again, believe it or not. She came to a Remembrance Service that Allen's parents and I held a couple of years after he vanished. Even though we had no way of knowing if he was dead or alive, we wanted to honor his memory. I hoped it would bring us some closure."

"That took some chutzpah, didn't it?" Neely asked.

"You can say that again. I was shocked, but not just because she had the gall to show up. Your question, Miriam, asking if she was still alive, triggered my memory of her appearance at the event. She and the guy she'd called Nick both turned up looking as if they were on their last legs. If I had any doubt about her drug use, it ended right then and there. From the volunteer work I've done with drug programs since then, I'd say they were the spitting image of meth addicts."

"Did she speak to you?"

"Oh, yes. She appeared to be genuinely sorry that Allen hadn't returned. Then, she made a pitch to me about how tough it had been to make ends meet since he took off."

"No way!" Joe exclaimed. "Did she ask you for money?"

"Not explicitly. If she had, I wouldn't have given it to her. I did express my concern that she didn't appear to be well, and then offered to drive her anywhere she was willing to go for help. She left soon after that."

"How about Allen's Army buddies? Did they show up

for the Remembrance Service?"

"No, not one of them. You know what, though? Now that we've been talking about all of this, Allen did go camping with them on occasion. Maybe they came here to the dunes area and the weekend he disappeared wasn't the first time. I'm sure I told the detective about Allen's friends from his service in Vietnam, but I don't believe I mentioned they could have been with him at the dunes. I never threw away my old address book. When I get home, I'll call and give you the contact information for the halfway house, the apartment complex where Allen was living, and the old information I had about Mark Viceroy and Allen's other Army buddies."

"Thanks," Charly said.

"It was such a long time ago, that I doubt the old information I have will be of much use to you. I drove by a couple of times long after Allen had disappeared, and the apartment complex had become more rundown, but it was still standing. Maybe there's some long-term tenant who remembers him, and might have something to contribute to your investigation. Please find out what happened to him and if his body really is buried somewhere on Dickens' Dune. He deserves better." She didn't say much more after that. I didn't know about her, but I was emotionally spent. Midge summarized the experience perfectly a few minutes later after we'd said goodbye to her.

"She certainly has taken Dickens' words seriously to 'have a heart that never hardens and a temper that never tires.' Her commitment to finding out what happened to her ex-husband, even after all she went through with him, is remarkable," Midge observed.

"I agree," Marty said. "I would have given up on him long ago. Then, I never knew the man."

"Okay, folks, we've got our work cut out for us," Charly said when she returned. "Who's going to do what?"

In a few minutes, we'd decided that Midge and Marty were going to Santa Barbara to speak to the nurse who'd heard Leonard Cohen's confession and relayed it to Judith. We hoped she might tell us if anyone visited Leonard Cohen while he was in the hospital—a spouse or child or some other family member. Even a friend who cared enough to visit him at the hospital.

Charly had a lot of background checks to run to get more information about Leonard Cohen and the other people Judith had mentioned who were close to Allen at the time he disappeared. In addition, she was going to get case files for Leonard Cohen and see if anyone else in Allen's circle of friends had a police record. Charly was working contacts in law enforcement in two County Sheriff Departments since Allen had lived in San Luis Obispo County, but disappeared here in the northernmost part of Santa Barbara County. That was in addition to other ties in the criminal justice system and the federal government she was using.

Carl and Joe were going to try to track down Mark Viceroy and speak to him if he was living in San Luis Obispo. They figured he might be more inclined to speak to a couple of "old guys" rather than "the ladies." While they were in the area, they also planned to make the rounds of veterans groups to see if anyone else remembered Allen Rogow, or better yet, had befriended him.

Neely and I were also going to San Luis Obispo after a quick stop at the public library in Duneville Down. We were going to make the rounds, visiting the halfway house—or rather, the version of it that was there now—decades later. We'd check out the apartment complex, and we'd try to speak to Wendy Ballard if she was still alive somewhere in the area. Rather than wait for Charly to get back to us with background information from her contacts, Neely and I both planned to troll the Internet for anything we could find about the key players identified so far in this mystery—Allen Rogow, Leonard Cohen, Wendy Ballard, and Mark Viceroy. I felt a little overwhelmed by all we had to do as we walked home with Emily and Domino in tow.

"Judith is the epitome of someone bent and broken into a better shape, isn't she? I suppose her strong faith has done that for her," I offered.

"Or the power of a first love," Charly suggested. I pondered how quickly that possibility had sprung to mind for her. Was it her devotion to the Brontë sisters and their gothic romances or was there an old love story in Charly's life that I hadn't heard about?

I was still pondering that question as Domino and I walked the block or so to the Hemingway Cottage. I was so engrossed in my own thoughts, that I never noticed a man anywhere nearby. Not until he spoke to me by name.

6

Self-swindlers

"All other swindlers on Earth are nothing to the self-swindlers, and with such pretenses did I cheat myself."

—Great Expectations

∞

"WELL, WELL, WELL, Miriam Webster, we meet at last!" As I turned, I searched the street for a car, wondering if we'd walked right past him. There wasn't a vehicle of any kind parked on the street. As I faced him, he closed the distance between us quickly.

He was breathing hard from the exertion, and I immediately recognized the hacking cough that overcame him for a moment. As he towered over me, I could smell his breath. It reeked of beer and cigarettes. When he moved his arm to adjust the sunglasses on his face, I could see that his fingertips were stained by nicotine—something I recognized from a short stint as a volunteer in a detox facility after the bakery shut down. There were lots of diehard smokers among clients at the drug facility. Unfortunately, I'd discovered I have a sensitivity to tobacco smoke—even second or third hand. I could feel my throat growing itchy.

"Who are you?" I replied as I took a step back and reached behind me for the gate that leads into my front yard. Domino didn't yield. In fact, she took a step toward the hulk of a man who was the same one I'd glimpsed at Dickens' Dune. I tightened my grip on Domino's leash as I heard a low growl come from her.

"Call off the dog. I'm here on business." When Domino growled again, he took a step back. After he'd spoken again, it was clear to me that his voice was the one I'd heard earlier on my phone.

"What sort of business?" I asked. I let out a tiny bit more of Domino's leash. She edged toward him, and he inched back. I slipped my other hand into a pocket and clutched the kubotan that Charly had given me soon after she'd used it so effectively at Shakespeare Cottage.

"Now, that's more like it—getting right to the point rather than dodging me and making me chase you down." He chuckled, and that set off a bout of coughing that made his bloodshot eyes water. "That climb up the dune, or whatever the dickens it is, nearly did me in!" Laughing at his own joke, set off another round of coughing. While he was wiping his eyes, I slipped my hand out of my pocket with the kubotan concealed in it.

"Do me a favor and get to the point, please." That brought him up short, and he went from garrulous to grim.

"Will do. Where's my money?"

"Money? What money?" I asked as my mind raced. He shook his head.

"Aw, come on. You can do better than that." My head spun, and I felt dizzy trying to fathom what he was talking about. "Pete said you were good for it or I never would have given him more money. Don't play dumb. Your signature is as plain as the nose on my face." He held out a sheet of paper in front of him. My mouth popped open when I saw a makeshift promissory note with my signature at the bottom of the page next to Pete's. It was typewritten on what was supposed to be letterhead, but I quickly spotted a misspelling and a couple of typos. That didn't stop me from feeling woozy again, this time as I peered at the dollar figure.

"Ten thousand dollars," I gasped.

"You do remember. Good! That's ten grand, plus penalties and interest. I should tag on the time and money I've spent tracking you down, too. By the time the loan came due, and I found out Pete was six feet under, you were long gone. I figured out where you'd gone and tried to pay you a visit at your apartment, but by then you'd left again! You're a sly one. Fast on your feet, too. I admire that in a woman, which is why I'm going to treat my expenses as part of the cost of doing business."

As he said that, he leered. Then he stuck a cigarette in his mouth and lit it. Something in the way he struck the match suddenly flipped a switch in my mind, and I remembered where I'd seen him before. He'd been standing in front of the building where Pete worked, chatting, and not in a casual way. When I'd pulled up to the curb to pick up Pete, I only caught a few words as they said goodbye. When Pete got into the car, I'd groused because he smelled like cigarette smoke.

"I don't get to tell my clients to quit smoking," he'd said in a casually, irritated fashion. Pete's tone and his reference to the man as a client had kept me from asking more questions. I hadn't seen the man's face, but his hulking form and mannerisms were enough to trigger the vague sense that I'd seen him somewhere before. The sick, uneasy feeling I get when I'm hit with some new revelation about Pete lying to me put me into a fog. The next words out of the man's mouth cleared it away.

"Let's make it twenty thou, okay? I'll tear up the promissory note, and we'll call it even." I wished that I'd snatched that paper away from him before he'd folded it and stuffed it into his shirt pocket behind his pack of cigarettes. I still held Domino's leash in one hand and my kubotan in the other.

"I can tell you right now that you've wasted your time. That's not my signature. I'm afraid Peter Webster deceived us both. If you want to take me to court, go ahead, but I'm not giving you any money." My heart was pounding in my throat, but I got the words out. He went from shocked to furious in seconds.

"I don't settle accounts in court, Miriam." He stepped forward and Domino lunged for him. She was furious now, too, barking and snapping as she jumped at him again. He stumbled as he stepped sideways to avoid her and then bent over awkwardly to regain his footing. Somehow, the pack of cigarettes dropped from his shirt pocket. When he leaned down to retrieve them, the bogus promissory note slipped out onto the sidewalk. I stepped on it, and he grabbed my ankle. I shifted my grip on the kubotan.

"Let go!" I said as I swung the keys and whacked him on the shoulder. He laughed but as his wheezing turned into coughing, he let go of my ankle, and Domino pounced on him before he could stand up. He tottered. With one more swing of my keys, I'd have him on the ground. Before I could move, someone leaned loud and long on a horn.

"Miriam!" a man shouted. We turned to see Joe and Carl run up onto the curb in a golf cart and stop. Edgar Humphrey, their passenger in the back seat, was the person who'd hollered my name.

"Call 911!" I shouted.

"Are you kidding me?" The guy asked as Carl and Joe climbed from the cart. I'll admit they didn't spring from the golf cart like Captain Marvel might have done, but Carl was armed, or so it appeared.

I knew it was a paintball gun and I hoped it was loaded because my would-be bill collector now held one of his own. Carl let it rip and hit the guy square in the face with a big blob of red paint that coated his sunglasses. He sputtered, spit paint, and ripped the sunglasses off. That was a mistake because paint from his forehead dribbled into his eyes.

Domino had his pant leg and yanked at him furiously. I heard his pants rip as he struggled to free his leg. His arm that still held the gun swung, aiming wildly. My aim wasn't wild, and the blow I delivered was on target this time. My keys hit him hard on the hand, he grunted loudly, and lowered his arm. Domino grabbed his sleeve, growling, and shook it hard enough that he dropped the gun.

As Joe scrambled for the gun, I heard sirens, and the thug took off. I grabbed Joe's arm before he could touch the gun. Edgar announced that he'd called 911 before I'd even asked him to do it.

"I gave them a description of the goon, too. That was before Carl plastered him with paint and Domino ripped his pants. It ought to be clear he doesn't belong in Seaview Cottages, so if he's got a car parked somewhere nearby, he'd better get to it in a hurry." The brute was lumbering in a half-blind kind of way.

"He was driving a rental car this morning. Charly and I gave the license plate number to the guard at the gate. That should have kept him out of here," I griped. Carl shook his head.

"Not necessarily. He could have easily traded in his rental car for another one since he knew you'd spotted him this morning, then parked at the clubhouse, and hiked over here."

"He doesn't strike me as the kind of guy who walks when he can ride. Maybe he's got a golf cart stashed on the next block," Joe suggested.

"Who knows? He appeared out of nowhere—no car engine or whirring golf cart. I'm sure he'll just put the extra expense on my tab." Then I gave them the two-minute version of what had gone on. "What do you want to bet the discount he offered me is no longer available?"

Cha-ching, I thought, as the sirens grew louder. The police had to be in the community by now.

"Good shot with the paintball gun," Joe added.

"Charly's Angels to the rescue," Carl said, bowing.

"We're probably going to be in for finger-wagging

when the police arrive, but what else could we have done? Thanks for the assist, you guys."

"Glad we could help, but you're no slouch with the kubotan. You've learned a thing or two from Charly," Joe commented. "Who was that dude?"

"I'm not sure. Hang on." I leaned over and picked up the folded piece of paper that was still nearby even though it had scooted free during the scuffle.

"Jimmy Dunn," I read aloud and then passed the paper to Carl.

"Phoniest piece of garbage I've seen in a long time. There's even a typo in the fake law office letterhead. I bet there's no such law firm anywhere in Ohio. I dealt with a ton of lawyers when I managed a collection agency. Lots of them had no head for numbers, but they understood a messy brief could get you laughed out of court. The terms of the agreement are laughable, too. What a swindler!"

"Jimmy Dunn's already told me he doesn't intend to take me to court to get the money he claims I owe him. My signature is as phony as the rest of the document. I don't doubt that Pete borrowed the money. He would have spotted those typos right away, so maybe Pete imagined he could wriggle out of repaying the loan given what a joke that promissory note is. At this point, it's not clear who was swindling whom."

"A couple of *self-swindlers*, if I can use another of the few phrases from Dickens that I recall. He sure got it right when he pointed out how many people who are out to swindle someone else, end up cheating themselves."

"You've got that right, Carl." Edgar's ruddy complexion flushed deeply, and he sounded angry as he spoke to me.

"If your husband imagined a few typos would let him wriggle out of a deal with Jimmy Dunn, he was a fool. Wriggle out of an alley on his belly, maybe, after the brute worked him over. Are you sure Pete died from natural causes?" Edgar asked. I opened my mouth to say "of course," and then shut it again. Something like an electric shock zipped through me.

"Pete dropped dead in front of his coworkers. They said it was a heart attack and the EMTs agreed. I was too out of it to question them. Maybe I should have asked for an autopsy, but it never occurred to me that someone murdered Pete. Stuff like that only happens to spies or crooks in books or movies, not to middle-aged couples living on a tree-lined street in an Ohio suburb."

"I'm sorry Pete didn't give more thought to the mess he was getting you into. Let's hope the police pick up Jimmy Dunn before he can make another attempt to collect the debt." I nodded wearily. My head hurt.

"Me, too, although I can't believe there won't be repercussions once the police get involved or I take that weasel to court and get a restraining order. Do any of you know a good lawyer? I might need one." I opened the gate and let Domino loose in the front yard. She must have felt I was no longer in danger because she immediately went to a favorite comfy chair on the porch.

"You bet I do—a whole carload of them, after all the trouble my son has had," Edgar assured me. "Howard's the poster boy for self-swindlers." Edgar shook his head, snorted, and then laughed. That turned into a coughing fit that was even worse than the one Jimmy Dunn had earlier.

Edgar, now in his nineties, had given up smoking years ago, but the damage was already done. He reached into the cart and got a small oxygen generator pack that he was probably supposed to be wearing. Once he attached the cannula and oxygen flowed, he breathed easily.

"I'm not sure why that poster boy comment made me laugh. Howard may be a self-swindler but he's no boy. That's not funny, is it? Sometimes you've got to laugh, so you don't cry." I knew exactly what he meant. He suddenly looked so downhearted I couldn't resist hugging him.

"You're the poster boy for dads who don't give up," I said. That made him happy or maybe it was the hug. When I turned around, Joe stood there with his arms out.

"Uh, no," I said. He shrugged and dropped his arms.

"It was worth a try," Joe added and grinned. "Listen! The sirens have stopped. Maybe they've got Jimmy Dunn cornered."

"The restraining order is a good idea. I'll give you the information for the firm I'm using in San Luis Obispo. Judith must use the same law firm because that's where I ran into her." I did a double-take.

"Not at the Community Center?" I asked. He looked puzzled, perhaps wondering why that mattered. I wasn't sure either, but I was now in full-blown paranoid mode after Jimmy Dunn had made it painfully clear that I probably should have asked more questions about what was up with Pete.

"We met there later for lunch, and that's when she told me an old friend claimed someone had murdered her ex-husband. Judith has a vacation condo at The Blue Haven

Resort and planned to drive down here to find someone who could help figure out what happened on Dickens' Dune. Charly had introduced me to Judith a while ago, so I told her to call and get the Grand Old Lady Detectives to help!"

"That was good advice. Go for the G.O.L.D.!" Joe exclaimed.

"In fact, I was on my way over here to tell you that Judith called to thank me for recommending she hire G.O.L.D. She raved about your coffee cake! When I saw Carl and Joe roaming the streets, I asked them if they wanted a lift. Judith really was happy to meet you all—even these clowns, if you can believe it."

"What Edgar's not telling you is that we saved his bacon before we saved yours. We warned him that his new health care aide was driving around in a car looking for him and then we switched seats. He's not allowed to drive—not even a golf cart!" Carl said.

"Yeah, he's lucky I got behind the wheel right before she caught up with him. She didn't look happy, but cruised on by when we waved at her."

"Sheila knows what she's doing, but she can be scary. Maybe I need to go with you, Miriam, and get a restraining order, too." Edgar guffawed and was on the verge of another attack as he drew in deep breaths of oxygen. Behind me, I heard a car coming or, more correctly, cars as I learned when Deputy Devers and Detective Hank Miller both pulled up at the curb. Behind them was a security patrol car. Doors slammed as they got out of their cars in a hurry.

"What the heck went on here?" Deputy Devers bellowed as he walked around his SUV and approached us.

"It's about time you showed up," Joe replied. "Some guy tried to strong-arm Miriam into giving him money. When she refused, he got mean." Joe pointed at the handgun on the ground.

"I'm the one who called 911 for help," Edgar explained. "Gave 'em a description, too, but he had to be easy to spot running down the street with big red splotches all over him after Carl shot him point blank with a paintball gun."

"Have you already hauled him off to the Duneville Down jail?" Carl asked as he peered into the deputy's backseat.

"The only place he's going is to the County Morgue," Devers replied. I gasped.

"What?" I asked. "Are you saying Jimmy Dunn is dead?" I directed that question to Hank who'd arrived looking plenty worried but hadn't uttered a word.

"He probably had a heart attack," Carl suggested. "By the way he was hacking up a lung when we drove up, Jimmy Dunn was not a well man."

"You can say that again. Running away like he did after chasing Miriam all the way up Dickens' Dune this morning must have been too much for him," Joe added.

"Serves him right!" Edgar exclaimed. "At least you won't need that restraining order now, will you?" Deputy Devers put both hands on his hips and shook his head.

"Will you stop second-guessing law enforcement? Jimmy Dunn didn't die from a heart attack. The driver of The Dunes Course beverage cart found him slumped over the wheel of a golf cart. The red splotches all over him aren't all paint since there's a bullet in his forehead."

The "this can't be real" feeling I'd experienced when Jimmy Dunn first accosted me on the street and demanded I fork over a small fortune hit me again. I must have wobbled because Hank reached out and grabbed my arm to steady me.

"Are you hurt?" Hank asked. "He didn't hit you, did he?" Words wouldn't come, but I shook my head no.

"Lucky for her we came along when we did, or she would have had to hurt him badly with her kubotan. That could have gotten ugly." Joe paused and then noticed that Domino was standing at the gate. "Domino was fired up, too, weren't you, girl?" She woofed and wiggled, no longer happy being confined in the front yard.

"From what Joe and Carl are saying, this is personal and not a problem related to the new case you've taken on, right?" Hank asked. I fought off tears and still couldn't speak. Instead, I nodded a sad, miserable yes in reply to Hank's question.

"Pffft! New case, right," Devers murmured.

"Darnell, make yourself useful and bag that weapon," Hank snapped. The deputy shuffled over to his SUV and pulled out what had to be a small evidence collection kit.

"That's not the one that killed him," Edgar said. "Miriam was right here with us the whole time and so was that gun. Joe and Carl can verify what I'm saying." That assertion got a thumbs-up from each man.

"That's Jimmy Dunn's cigarette butt, too," I added pointing to where the lowlife had dropped it when he fled. "There might be a small piece of cloth from his shirt or pants around here somewhere. Domino did her best to rip off his clothes. And then there's this." I held up the bogus promissory note. It was dirty, crumpled, and had part of a footprint on it.

"That's my footprint, and, as you can see, I've handled it. Obviously, my fingerprints will be all over it, too."

"Mine, too," Carl added. "We didn't know the culprit was going to get himself killed, and you'd need it as evidence in a murder inquiry." While Deputy Devers fumbled around putting on a pair of gloves and slipping items into evidence bags, Hank read the note. When he got to the bottom line, he glanced at me.

"Not my signature," I said before he could ask. "I caught a glimpse of Jimmy Dunn with Pete once, but my husband lied and told me he was a client, not a loan shark." Hank looked at me, and I saw sympathy rather than suspicion in his eyes, which was a huge relief.

"Well, it's a lot of money. I'm guessing Jimmy Dunn was more the legman than the financier. He had to be in deep trouble for someone to kill him—bigger trouble than coming up with the money he loaned Pete." Hank suggested. "A guy like him must have had a few run-ins with the law. Maybe his criminal record will hint at who he's fronting."

"Whoever he's working for was really unhappy with his work performance," Joe commented. "A bullet is a heck of a termination notice!"

"Let's hope they don't deal with debtors that way, too." A pit had formed in my stomach to go with the pulsing in my head.

"They won't get back their money that way. Rough you up, yes. Kill you, I doubt it. If you were the target of a hit, you'd already be dead." I stared at the deputy trying to gauge if he was serious, or merely toying with me.

"Thanks, Darnell. I'll try to keep that in mind when they're only roughing me up."

"Look, it's too soon to draw any conclusions about who killed Jimmy Dunn or why. Darnell has a point that loan sharks can't get back their money if they kill the person who borrowed it. They don't usually go around breaking people's legs either—at least not until they've tried scaring money out of them first. This was Jimmy Dunn's first attempt to get you to pay up, right?" I frowned.

"Of course, it is. If Jimmy Dunn had asked me for money while I was still in Ohio, I would have contacted my cousin, Kevin, who's on the police force. There would have been no need for him to travel all the way to California to track me down. I saw the guy once, with Pete, a couple of years ago!"

"Did he see you?" Hank asked.

"I don't know. I was in my car, in the driver's seat. He could have caught a glimpse of me. I never noticed him after that, but maybe he was following Pete around to keep an eye on him. I doubt that, though, since he said he didn't try to get his money back from Pete until after he was dead."

"Once he got here, it would have been easy enough to find her. She and her old lady friends are out on the dunes almost every morning walking their dogs."

I cocked my head, wondering how the deputy was so sure he had that right. Then I remembered Chef Tony griping that the cheapskate frequently hit him up for free coffee and a piece of the pie of the day at the restaurant in the clubhouse.

"Are you stalking us, Deputy?" I asked, raising one eyebrow. As Devers sputtered, Hank squelched a smile.

"It's a joke, Darnell. Lighten up."

"In his own special way, Darnell is making a good point. You ought to lie low for a couple of days while we sort this out. If Darnell has figured out your routine, someone else could do it too. Why not go visit one of your friends for a few days?"

"Are you telling me to get out of Dodge, Detective? If so, I'm way ahead of you. I already have plans to leave town for a few days."

"You'd better make sure you keep us informed of your whereabouts," Darnell responded.

"We're going too, so you won't have us to kick around for a while either," Carl and Joe added. Darnell frowned.

"Aw, he's going to miss you, isn't he?" Edgar asked in a wheezy tone. He looked tired despite his attempt to stir up a little trouble. Before anyone could say more, a call came in. Devers ran to his SUV to hear what the dispatcher was saying. Hank took a call on his cellphone. He gave my hand a squeeze.

"Take Edgar home," Hank said.

"Miriam, you and Domino go inside. Lock the doors. I'll call you later." Then he and Darnell took off.

7

A Secret to Each Other

"A wonderful fact to reflect upon, that every human creature is constituted to be that profound secret and mystery to every other."
—A Tale of Two Cities

∞

AS SOON AS Domino and I were inside with the doors locked and the security alarm set, I fixed a cup of Chamomile tea and called Charly. I filled her in on the latest debacle. Once I'd given her the details that included the murder of Jimmy Dunn, I ranted about Pete.

"Are you really all that surprised?" She asked.

"Yes, I am. I was married to Pete for more than twenty-five years, and, apparently, I never knew him."

"Dickens makes a terrifyingly astute observation about that in *A Tale of Two Cities.* He says that as humans, we're predisposed to be a profound secret and a mystery to each other. Why would Pete have been an exception?" Charly paused before going on. "Maybe Pete hid things from you that he thought would hurt you, or that would diminish him in your eyes."

"Getting mixed up with a goon like Jimmy Dunn was hurtful whether Pete hid it from me or not," I snapped. Then I paused, remembering the worry on Pete's face. It hadn't always been there. It never stayed there long, but a more perceptive person might have asked more questions. "He wasn't always secretive. Maybe losing my job was more of a burden on him than I realized. I never expected him to carry the load."

"From what you've told me about Pete, I'd say his troubles stemmed more from his high-spirited nature and wild ambitions than from concern about the job you lost."

"The go-getter in him was certainly part of what made him so successful in his sales position. His company was sad that he died because everyone liked him as a person. Pete's boss also admitted that losing Pete was going to be bad for their bottom line. Being so highly regarded in his job must not have been enough for Pete. If only he could have told me how much more he wanted to achieve, maybe I could have helped him figure out how to do it. No matter what Dickens said, love is about sharing secrets, letting your guard down, and striving not to remain a mystery, isn't it?"

"Miriam, you're even more of a romantic than I am."

"I doubt it. On days like today, I wonder if I would have been better off without love or marriage." As I said that, Hank's handsome face appeared before me. My heart had skipped a beat when he squeezed my hand—even in the middle of the mess created by the late, inscrutable Peter Webster.

Maybe I am a hopeless romantic, I thought.

"Losing Pete was bad, but his betrayal is worse—it's

like losing him all over again. The guilt is overwhelming, too, since I feel as if I was a co-conspirator, keeping his secrets even though I didn't know I was doing it."

"Your accountant should have been more forthcoming with you before Pete died. Waiting until you became a widow to tell you he suspected your husband had 'gotten creative,' and gone off the books with your finances wasn't helpful."

"Pete was feeding him papers with my signature on them, so I believe he was genuinely surprised I was as out of the loop as I was. The bigger question I have is, why didn't I know?"

"Judith Rogow has asked me almost the same thing. She also said it's the secrets we don't know we're keeping that can be the most dangerous. I'm sure that's one of the main reasons she's still pushing to get closure. If you're okay with it, why don't I see what I can find out about Peter Webster?"

"Why not? Break it to me gently, will you?" I responded after pausing to consider what her offer might mean. "Hank is going to check into Jimmy Dunn's background and will tell us what he finds out about that mad man. I'm sorry to have this bomb go off right in the middle of our efforts to solve the mystery of Allen Rogow's disappearance."

"Actually, it's good that you have work to do so you don't let your mind run wild. Whoever financed Pete's loan may want the money back, but I agree with what Hank already told you about Jimmy Dunn. You don't need a background check to figure out he was up to his neck in trouble, which only incidentally had anything to do with you."

"I hear you. Darnell was being a jerk when he said it, but I hope he was right that if there was a hit out on me, I'd already be dead." I sighed. I felt relieved hearing Charly's reassurance. She was right, too, about the importance of staying busy.

"A change of scene will do you good. Find a place to stay on the beach and see the sights while you and Neely are in San Luis Obispo. One of Father Serra's old California missions is there and, if you have time, the Hearst Castle is an interesting place up the coast a little farther north."

"Hank said something like that, too. It wasn't 'get out of town by sundown,' but it was close."

"Hank is worried about you, that's all. You'll be safer not roaming the streets around here while they get a handle on what the heck is going on with Jimmy Dunn."

"Depending on how fast we get our sleuthing tasks done, I'll talk to Neely about playing tourists. I'd love to see more of the area. Is there anything I should share with her in the way of updates?" I asked.

"As a matter of fact, there is," Charly responded. Wendy Ballard is dead. If it's true that Allen Rogow was murdered in 1982, she didn't outlive him by much. It probably won't surprise you that she had a police record."

"As in drug violations?"

"Yes. Wendy Ballard spent a few days in jail the second time she was arrested for possessing small amounts of barbiturates and marijuana."

"Not methamphetamines as Judith suspected?"

"There's no formal charge related to meth, but who

knows what drugs she was taking? She did a stint in rehab as a guest of the county in an effort at diversion. That's not unusual for a drug offender. What is interesting is that Wendy Ballard had a nasty temper. She'd refused treatment as an alternative to jail time on the drug charge, but agreed to go to rehab when she was later charged with assault."

"Who charged her with assault?"

"Nick Martinique, the housemate Judith mentioned, took a bad blow to the head when he and Wendy got into a row while they were both under the influence of alcohol and other drugs. He didn't call the police, but the neighbors did. They claimed it wasn't the first time she and Nick had gone at it. On another occasion, Wendy had taken a swing at a neighbor who complained about how she'd parked, and another time someone saw her slap a man who walked with a limp. That could have been Allen Rogow."

"Aha! So, she could have killed him if she was angry and stoned enough."

"I'd say it's entirely possible. I'm not sure how much she learned from her stint in drug treatment either. Not long after she completed rehab, she was picked up for a DUI. She served thirty days of a ninety-day jail sentence until someone paid her fine for her. Guess who?" Hearing the tone in her voice, an image of Charly as a cartoon cat that had swallowed the canary suddenly appeared.

"Not Allen Rogow?"

"No, his buddy, Mark Viceroy."

"Now, that's very interesting. Why would he care one way or another if Wendy Ballard was in jail?" I wondered aloud.

"That's one of the first questions that popped into my head. And, I may have found someone who can tell us. Wendy Ballard died of a drug overdose two years after Allen disappeared. Her friend, Nick Martinique, is still alive though. He left the area shortly after Wendy died, but his name shows up again, years later, with an address in San Luis Obispo."

"Judith said she saw them at that remembrance service around that time. Wendy must have been as bad off as Judith thought she was. Does that seem odd to you that he left town? Was there anything suspicious about Wendy Ballard's death?"

"That's a good question. I got the information about her from a death certificate completed by the Santa Barbara General Hospital. She died in their emergency room, so they may have done an autopsy, which should have reported any unusual findings to the police. If not, there may not be much more in the official records. Medical records are private, and California only requires that they are kept for seven years."

"I'm a little surprised Wendy Ballard didn't die in a San Luis Obispo hospital. Midge is going to be in Santa Barbara tomorrow. Given how much she gets around, I bet she has contacts with hospital personnel who were around back then, even if they're retired now. It's a long shot, but maybe someone can recall if there were any unusual circumstances surrounding Wendy Ballard's death."

"Long shot is right. Not only did her death occur eons ago, but addicts die in emergency rooms all the time. I need to touch base with Midge and share these updates with her. She may have some other strategies for finding a needle in a haystack."

"In the meantime, Neely and I will do our best to track down Nick Martinique. Let's see what he can tell us about how his friend died. He might be able to tell us what she was doing in Santa Barbara."

"Good! The most recent address for him is in Pismo Beach. That's about fifteen minutes south of San Luis Obispo. If you can't locate him there, you might try speaking to someone at his place of employment—The Maiden Inn. It's an old historic inn where he's a night manager."

"Isn't he retired by now?"

"Apparently, not. It's listed as his 'current employer.' He was barely out of his teens when he showed up at that memorial service for Allen with Wendy Ballard. Although from the way Judith described him, he may have appeared much older. If he and Wendy were addicted to methamphetamine, it wouldn't be unusual if they both looked older than they were. He's not sixty yet, so there's a good chance he's still on duty at The Maiden Inn."

"If you're right, Neely and I might have a better chance of contacting him by just showing up there."

"It's worth a try, Miriam. He's probably at home sleeping if he's on duty all night. Nick Martinique might prefer to speak to you at work rather than have his sleep interrupted during the daytime."

"Okay, I'm going to call Neely and share all this info with her. I'll see if she's willing to stay an extra day to make sure we have the time to do everything we've planned. If we get it all done without using the extra day, we'll do the sightseeing you recommend." I was about to say goodbye when I had another thought. "If Nick's willing to talk, maybe he can tell us how to find Mark Viceroy—unless you already know where he is."

"Not yet. His record is even spottier than Nick Martinique's is. Some of the gaps are related to jail time and a long prison stint—not in The Men's Colony where Allen Rogow and Leonard Cohen spent time, but Calipatria State Prison in Blythe."

"Is there a reason he ended up there rather than in The Men's Colony?"

"Yes. Apparently, Mark Viceroy was something of an escape artist and managed to get out of jail twice before he was sent to prison. The second time he succeeded in getting away, he eluded police for almost ten years. He was originally sentenced to serve two years for selling drugs, and another year for having an unregistered handgun in his possession when he was arrested. When they finally caught up with him years later, they added more time for the escape and for assaulting a guard in the process."

"If he was hiding out from the authorities, it's no wonder his public record is spotty. Even with all the time added on he must have been released years ago."

"But wait—there's more! Mark Viceroy had trouble adjusting to prison life at Calipatria. After only serving a year of his eight-year sentence, he made another escape attempt. He and four other inmates stabbed eight prison guards in the process, nearly killing one of them. That added attempted murder to his record. He served the remainder of his sentence housed in maximum security, with few privileges, until he was finally released a year ago." I still had goosebumps when I responded to Charly.

"Go to the head of the class of suspects, Mark Viceroy!" I exclaimed. "He just shoved Wendy Ballard out of the way as my nominee for 'most likely to have succeeded' at murdering a friend. Allen Rogow sure knew how to pick them, didn't he?"

"I agree. Mark Viceroy strikes me as the kind of person whose troubles with authority could have started while he was a member of the armed forces. He gets a nomination from me as the person Allen was referring to when he let it slip that he was paying a price for trusting the wrong people."

"One of them maybe since, if Judith is remembering correctly, he did say people and not person."

"That's a good point, Miriam. We should all keep that in mind. Call me if you find out why Hank and Darnell took off like that. Don't wait if you and Neely come up with something that's important. It's going to be a few days before we can get together to debrief, so I'm going to try to play coordinator while you're all out on assignment."

"Will do!" As I ended the call and dialed Neely, I was suddenly engulfed by a new wave of paranoia. Was Jimmy Dunn's killer stalking me? What had caused Hank and Darnell to take off like that when that call came in? If Mark Viceroy was still alive, would he come after us if we started asking questions about him? What about Nick Martinique? Was it a coincidence that he left the area so soon after Wendy Ballard overdosed, or did he leave because he was somehow involved in her death?

8

An Uncommon Man

"If you can't get to be uncommon through going straight, you'll never get to do it through going crooked."

—Great Expectations

∞

I HAD A restless night, dreaming about being spied on and stalked. The person doing the stalking switched from one person to another. A zombie version of Jimmy Dunn, who'd come back to life was creepy, but the gun-toting Deputy Devers wasn't much better. Most unnerving of all was a shadowy figure with burning eyes peering from behind a bush. When I couldn't go back to sleep, I gave up and got up before the alarm went off. Domino was delighted until I let her out into the backyard instead of taking the hint from the leash that she'd brought me.

"Later, girl. Momma's got herself into another mess. Neely gave us very specific guidelines to follow this morning, and we're going to do it." That included making sure Domino had her playtime in the back yard. If anyone was keeping an eye on me, she wanted to make sure they caught a good look at the spirited spotted dog I'd had with me at Dickens' Dune.

"If someone was following him while he was following you, Domino had to be a standout. Let's make sure they see her, know which cottage you live in, and what car you drive." That had seemed odd until she'd spilled the beans.

"Hank's going to send a woman police officer to play decoy for you tomorrow. Once you get to my cottage, she's going to drive out of here in your car, dressed like you, and accompanied by a gorgeous Dalmatian."

"How will she get Domino back to me?"

"You don't need to worry about that. Domino's going to have a decoy, too. Officer Clemons has borrowed a Dalmatian from a Dalmatian rescue shelter. If Jimmy Dunn's killer takes the bait, she should have someone tailing her in no time. Hank suggested it might be a good idea to prepare for the eventuality that she'll stay at your house for a night or two."

After a breakfast that included extra coffee, I showered and dressed as I'd been instructed. When I recalled more of my conversation with Neely from the evening before, a strange flush stole over me. I'd been flattered and irked at the same time as Neely filled me in on the scheme she and Hank had discussed.

"Hank sure has a good memory," I'd said. "I've only worn the outfit he's describing once, and he's remembered every detail."

"The man's a detective, and he's taken a special interest in the latest entanglement for a woman whose neck he's trying to save. It's lucky for you he has such vivid recall of the outfit you had on since those details are important in transforming your doppelganger into a convincing copy of you."

"Well, I'm sorry he's put you to so much trouble." Neely had chuckled when I said that. My irritation had won out. Why hadn't Hank just called me? She read my mind.

"In case you were wondering, Hank would have called and told you all about this himself, but he needed to read me in as his co-conspirator. Besides, he didn't want to give you any chance to object, and I agreed." I hadn't bothered to argue with her at that point.

In the clear light of day, I could see she and Hank were right. I spent the morning readying my house for a guest, which included cooking and baking to soothe my frazzled nerves. Then I packed as I'd been instructed to do. Mid-afternoon, I loaded the car and added a red baseball cap and sunglasses to my ensemble. By then, I was eager to meet my twin and get on with their scheme.

"Let's go meet Momma's doppelganger, Domino. Yours too!" She cocked her head to one side and then the other before hopping into the back seat for me to strap her into her harness.

The drive to Neely's house was a short one, but I kept checking my rearview mirror in case I was being followed. I didn't see a soul on the street in a car or on foot. The HOA discourages residents from parking on the street, so there weren't more than a couple of cars parked along the blocks I covered. A golf cart or two, as well, but that was it.

"Maybe Detective Miller has become as paranoid as me, Domino," I muttered as I pulled into Neely's driveway. As I sat there, a white hatchback drove by and appeared to slow down a bit. I was on the verge of panic when Neely's garage door rose. When I looked in my rearview mirror, the car was gone.

In addition to dressing in a specific way and bringing Domino with me, I'd been instructed to pack my belongings for our travels in nondescript boxes and bags rather than luggage. I loaded the items onto the little wheeled cart I'd used the few times I'd catered events. I rolled everything in through the garage door Neely had opened which she shut as soon as Domino and I were inside.

"I hope the hotel in Pismo Beach doesn't mind a bag lady checking in!"

"Don't worry. I've got you covered. You'll have to repack, but it won't take long to transfer what you've brought into my extra suitcases. I have a set I received as swag at a Hollywood movie party, and I've never even used them. Come in and meet Miriam Webster and Domino, Version 2.0."

I walked into Neely's kitchen and stopped in my tracks when I came face-to-face with my double. The resemblance was uncanny, as she stood there wearing my outfit with a Dalmatian at her side. Then Officer Clemons shoved the dark glasses she wore up on top of her head and spoke. She was half my age and had the distinctive lilt to her voice I'd heard often even before arriving on the West Coast. Her "Valley Girl" accent wasn't as exaggerated as some used by actresses in movies, but it was impossible to miss.

"I'm happy to meet you, Ms. Webster. Hank Miller has told me so much about you. That's in addition to the news coverage you've recently received. I'm Officer Denver Clemons," she said as she stepped forward and stuck out her hand. I must have had a puzzled expression on my face. Denver struck me as an unusual name for a woman who'd obviously grown up in California.

"My dad was a sports fanatic. It's Denver as in the Denver Broncos. It's better than Bronco Clemons!" When she smiled, her eyes danced, and I was instantly won over by her good humor.

"Call me Miriam, please, Denver. Thanks for your help. This must be an odd assignment!"

"So far, it's been an easy one. I haven't had much opportunity to do undercover work, so it's a welcome change of pace. Besides, Mr. Handsome, here, has been an awesome pal to have around. I wish I could keep him, but I live in a tiny apartment in Santa Maria. Pets aren't welcome. I had to sneak him into my place last night. Domino seems pleased to meet him." Domino's tail was wagging wildly, and the two dogs had exchanged friendly woofs the moment they spotted each other.

"Fleck, say hello to Miriam." The dog stepped forward and offered me his paw, which I shook. "He's obviously a friendly, well-trained dog. His foster mom took him in after his family lost their home in a fire."

"It's a pleasure to meet you, Fleck," I said. That greeting earned me a woof, and a friendly nuzzle.

"So, what happens now?" I asked as I dug out treats for the adorable pair of spotted dogs. They were very similar in appearance although Fleck was larger than Domino. I handed Neely a container. "Treats for us," I said before giving Denver a chance to respond.

"I can tell you what I'm doing next," Neely said. "We're having a cup of tea, unless you'd prefer coffee, Denver. Mm, and with doughnuts in honor of our special guest, huh? They're no ordinary doughnuts, are they?" She asked as their aroma hit her.

"Earl Grey doughnuts with a brown butter glaze," I responded.

"Those look amazing," Denver added as Neely let her peek at them. "Tea and doughnuts are a great idea. Once we've established that you stopped by and dropped off a few things for your friend, you're going to run errands. I'll leave here in your car." She paused, eying those doughnuts as Neely set them out on a plate and poured tea for us.

"My plan is to take Fleck to a park for a run and then drive to Duneville Down, fill up the tank at the truck stop just off the highway, and then visit several stores. My partner is waiting near the guard gate. He'll follow me to see if I pick up a tail. He won't wait until anyone approaches me. If he spots the same car anywhere near me more than once, he'll call in the plates, and someone in a patrol car will have a chat with the driver. We don't want to do anything to blow my cover if I need to play this out for another day or two." She smiled again and patted Fleck's head. "I hope it wasn't too inconvenient preparing for last minute guests."

"Less trouble than being hassled by Jimmy Dunn or ending up the way he did." Denver laughed as Neely led us to the kitchen table, and we slipped into chairs.

"I can understand that. He sure fits the profile of a wise guy, doesn't he?"

"As in mobster?" I asked, glancing at Neely. Denver

nodded, but couldn't speak since she'd taken a bite of the doughnut on her plate. Neely shrugged as she chomped on her doughnut. Apparently, Hank hadn't let her in on everything they found out about my dead stalker.

"Good grief! I thought Darnell was being ridiculous when he talked about someone putting out a hit on me. You'll take care of Domino if I end up like Jimmy Dunn, won't you, Neely?" That struck Denver as funny, and she laughed heartily.

"Honestly, I doubt the Ohio mob would chase you all the way to California for the ten thousand dollars your husband borrowed. If I had to make a guess, I'd say Jimmy Dunn was on the run, tracked you down to see if he could squeeze you for a quick twenty K on his way to Mexico. Maybe, he was already in the area when your name and face were splashed all over the media after the murder of Shakespeare's ghost."

"He wasn't a very smart wise guy, was he?" Neely asked. "If Pete could have gotten his hands on that kind of money, why would he have borrowed money from the likes of Jimmy Dunn?"

"Jimmy Dunn might have figured you'd ended up with money from your husband's life insurance and wanted a cut," Denver suggested.

"Pete borrowed against that, too. I'm afraid my husband had more ambition than brains in his effort to escape his humdrum life at the cost of dealing with crooks."

"You know what Dickens had to say about that." Denver and I both shook our heads no. "It's from *Great Expectations*: *If you can't get to be uncommon through going straight, you'll never get to do it through going crooked.*"

"I wouldn't have put it so eloquently, but I could have told him that if Pete had let me in on his secrets. I could have sworn that his common sense would have made it clear to him without needing to say it. He was always an uncommon man to me." I looked away as tears welled up in my eyes.

"Well, I doubt Jimmy Dunn would have been wise enough to get the point even if Dickens himself had told him that. He must have been plenty desperate to accost you in broad daylight. All this cloak and dagger stuff is insurance against the possibility that we're wrong about Dunn, or that Dunn's killer is in 'might as well' mode." I stared at her blankly. "You know, 'I've come all this way to put an end to Jimmy Dunn's worthless life so I might as well shake down Pete's widow for the money he borrowed.'"

"No one ever mentioned there'd be such a high price to pay for my fifteen minutes of fame," I groaned.

"I'm sure Hank has other angles he's working," Neely said, patting my arm.

"True. Hank may have a lead on the woman who was with Dunn at Dickens' Dune, despite the fact you didn't get a good look at her. If Jimmy Dunn's killer is any smarter than his target, he'll already have slinked back to wherever he came from before getting his fifteen minutes of fame. They got a look at him on some surveillance camera, and someone thought they spotted him near The Blue Haven Resort, but it didn't pan out."

"Did that happen yesterday soon after they found Jimmy Dunn in the golf cart?" I asked. She nodded, yes. At least I now knew why Hank and Darnell had taken off at a sprint, but it's too bad the culprit was still at large.

"Please tell me there are more of these doughnuts at your house," Denver added, changing the subject.

"Yes, there are. I'm sorry Domino and I can't be there to make sure you're comfortable. I've posted my cellphone number along with the information about our hotel in Pismo Beach. I'm sure the constabulary can track me down if your questions are about the police investigation, but feel free to call me on my cellphone if you can't find a can opener or if something breaks down. I can solve that problem quicker than the police can. Here's the code for the security system—you've got ninety seconds to punch it in before the alarm sounds."

"Is there a good pizza place that delivers?" Denver asked.

"The number for pizza delivery is on a list of numbers for local eateries I frequent on occasion, along with the drug store and pharmacy I use, my grocery store, the post office, and Domino's vet in case Fleck needs attention. There's a pasta salad in the fridge for dinner, fresh-baked muffins for breakfast, and treats for Fleck in a little plastic container on the kitchen island. Make yourself at home in the guest room. Fleck should too. Dogs are allowed on the furniture."

"Wow! You've thought of everything. Your baking is legendary. Hank's sure no dummy. He told me you'd probably leave me treats. He knows you pretty well, doesn't he?" I felt a warm rush of gratitude mixed in with the embarrassment Denver's smirk induced.

"Given all the trouble we've been in, he probably knows me better than he ever dreamed he would when we first met. Poor man," I said.

"Don't feel sorry for him. The word on the street is that he's in a better mood than he's been in for years. I've also heard it's more than the sugar in the sweets you bake, that's done that." She beamed that good-natured smile at me again. Then she abruptly stood, took her cup and plate to the kitchen sink. "Time to get this show on the road. Hank will call you if there are any important developments. I'm supposed to tell you to enjoy your getaway and stay out of trouble. Hank's authority doesn't extend to San Luis Obispo."

I placed the keys to my house and car into the hand Denver held out. She slipped on the sunglasses and a bright red baseball cap and led Fleck to the front door. Domino whined when I held her by the collar to keep her from dashing after Denver and her new best friend, Fleck. We followed at a distance. On the porch, Neely and Denver played out the part of two friends saying a quick goodbye before Denver got into my car that I'd left in the driveway.

We cleaned up Neely's kitchen and repacked my belongings in the suitcases Neely had dragged out. Then Neely insisted that I take one more precaution by donning a blond wig before we left for Pismo Beach in her car. Domino did as I asked and lay in her harness sprawled out on the backseat until we were in Pismo Beach. She needed a nap after racing back and forth with Fleck in Neely's hallway. Even disguised as a blonde with no spotted doggie taking in the view, I kept a watchful eye on the road. Being an afterthought or a "might as well" wasn't any better in my book than being a hitman's primary target.

9

An Innocent Man?

"Circumstances may accumulate so strongly even against an innocent man, that directed, sharpened, and pointed, they may slay him."
—The Mystery of Edwin Drood

∞

IT TOOK US less than an hour to make the drive from Seaview Cottages to Pismo Beach. When Neely pulled up in front of one of the swankiest resorts I'd ever seen, my mouth dropped open. I'd visited the Ritz Carlton in Cleveland for a conference, but I'd stayed at a much less expensive hotel a few blocks from the conference site.

"What are you doing?" I asked. "I made reservations for us at the Schooner Inn."

"I know. I canceled them and booked us into a suite here. We'll have privacy, but it'll be easier to keep an eye on you if we're in the same suite. I promised Hank I'd do that. They're pet-friendly, and they owe me."

"When you say, 'they owe you,' what does that mean?" As Neely replied, valets descended upon us.

"In my Hollywood days, I steered lots of business their

way. Santa Barbara is a favorite getaway for Hollywood's 'talent,' but the nice places there were often booked. I scouted out this place for an agent friend of mine, and that put them 'on the map,' so-to-speak." She nonchalantly shrugged as I continued to stare at her. It had taken me a little while, but I'd begun to realize that Neely's connections via her days as a Hollywood makeup artist were about as extensive as those Charly had established with law enforcement and Midge with the regional health care system.

"Thank goodness, I didn't show up with my belongings in cardboard boxes and garbage bags." As I said that, someone opened my door for me, and a woman in an expensive-looking blue sleeveless dress and spiky heels darted toward us.

"Neely, darling! How wonderful to see you!" Neely slid out from behind the wheel and hugged the woman. It was a real hug, not just an exchange of "air kisses."

"It's good to see you, too, Chelsea. This is my friend I told you about," Neely said, waving her hand my way. "Miriam Webster, this is Chelsea Glen, one of the head honchos around here."

"How nice to meet you," Chelsea said as she swooped toward me. "That must be Domino! What a gorgeous Dalmatian." Domino woofed in approval of the compliment. We were swept up in a whirlwind of motion as the woman issued directives to valets, bellhops, and even a "handler" for pets. I stopped as we entered the spectacular lobby. The ocean view was breathtaking, even though I admire the blue Pacific Ocean every day from my cottage porch.

If we'd had any hope of keeping a low profile, that was gone as everyone turned to gauge what was causing all the commotion. I heard oohs and ahs as they caught sight of Domino. She was stepping beside her handler like a dressage pony.

A member of hotel security joined our entourage. He escorted us directly to an elevator without stopping at one of the tables designated as a place to check in. In minutes, we were in our suite, which seemed as big as my cottage. That wasn't true, of course, but the wall of windows made the accommodations appear to be even larger than they were.

Domino ran from one room to another. While Neely issued instructions to the baggage handlers, I followed Domino into my bedroom. She immediately found a doggie bed with toys in it. She probably wouldn't sleep in the bed, but a squeaky toy was an instant hit. A valet set my suitcase on a luggage stand, put my overnight bag in the bathroom, and hung up my dress bag. After thanking and tipping him, there really wasn't much for me to do, except try out the bed. Domino thought that was an invitation to do the same as she bounced and rolled on it a couple of times before taking off again.

"Domino is so wound up. Do you want to go with me to let her run off some energy on the beach?" Domino was lapping water from a silver bowl in the kitchen. Her tail whipped wildly at the mention of her name in the same breath as beach. "How do you like that? They've stocked her usual kibble, thank you very much!"

"No detail is overlooked, my dear. That's one of the reasons the darlings of Hollywood come back again and again. It's a great idea to let Domino wear herself out. Then we need to get cleaned up for dinner. I made reservations for us so we can get our investigation underway."

"Don't tell me—dinner for two at The Maiden Inn, right?"

"Yes. I hope we can recognize Nick Martinique, although we could just ask to speak to the night manager. Charly sent me an old photo from his case file. What a wreck he was in his mug shot. I find it hard to believe he's still alive."

"Oh, he is," I asserted. "I went through every picture I could find in any post on the Internet about The Maiden Inn. I found him. See?"

"When did you have time to do that?" Neely asked as she scanned the group photo on my cellphone with the names of employees written underneath it.

"Last night when I couldn't sleep. I downloaded others, but this one's only a couple of years old." She studied the photo of a thin, bespectacled man, with a shock of white hair.

"He looks better there than he did a couple of decades earlier. We'll have no trouble identifying him. Bravo, Miriam!"

"Let's go to the beach so we won't be late for dinner," I said. "I can't wait to hear what Nick Martinique has to say about Wendy Ballard and Allen Rogow."

"If we can get him to talk about it. I've been trying to come up with a strategy for approaching him. We could be direct, but since Wendy Ballard died from an overdose, that has to be a touchy subject even after all these years."

I put Domino on her leash as I spoke and led her out into the hallway. We had the elevator all to ourselves when it arrived, and Neely who'd been deep in thought, finally weighed in on the matter as the elevator descended.

"We could use the old 'mother-daughter' routine," Neely suggested. "You know—you're in the area checking it out as a place to open a bake shop. Does someone at The Maiden Inn do their baking or do they have a shop they already use?"

"Something like that might get the conversation started in a non-threatening way. I'm not sure how we get to the point. 'By the way, we're wondering if your friend, Wendy Ballard, killed Allen Rogow before she overdosed.' I can already see the back of his head as he retreats."

"Well, maybe we could drop Judith Rogow's name as a person who recommended we speak to him given his employment in the local service industry. Although, the mere mention of her name might be enough to send him running."

As she said that, the elevator stopped, and Domino darted out the instant the doors opened pulling me after her. She was agile enough to avoid the gentleman standing there. I was not and bumped into him with my nose barely an inch away from his chest.

"I am so sorry," I said, as I backed away from the clean-shaven man who smelled of a fresh, ocean-y fragrance. He smiled as I backed into the elevator door that was closing, and reached around me to catch it. It slid open again and he turned sideways, allowing me to escape while he held it open.

"Please don't apologize. I was in too big a hurry and

should have waited to make sure the elevator was empty. What a pleasant surprise to see such a lovely creature emerge so energetically." A friendly smile went with that comment.

"Thank you. She can be a little too energetic, but Domino is a lovely girl." He turned to smile at Domino, who was now sitting at Neely's side like a perfect angel.

"Her, too!" He said as he turned back to me. "Allow me to introduce myself. I'm Ricardo Cantinela, and you are?" For an instant, I froze. Then, for some reason, I lied.

"I'm Miriam. Miriam Ingram," I said. "That's my mother Cornelia, but everyone calls her Neely." I was going to use the names Neely had made up for us the last time we'd played mother and daughter, but I couldn't quite remember what they were. What I did remember was how easily our scheme unraveled once we ran into someone who'd used our real first names.

"It's a pleasure to meet you both. I must apologize again for being in such a rush. Perhaps, the next time we bump into each other, I won't have to leave so quickly. Au revoir!" With that, he stepped into the elevator and hit a button. I heard the doors close as I led Domino out a side door that I hoped would take us to the beach.

"I would have expected 'adios' or 'ciao' from a man named Ricardo Cantinela. Quick thinking not to give out our last names without checking him out first. I'm sending Charly his name right now, along with a description. Those blue eyes were stunning in contrast to his black hair, weren't they?" I nodded although I doubt Neely saw it. I was pondering the encounter and trying to understand why I'd lied so blithely.

Ricardo Cantinela couldn't have been more charming or polite. Neely was right about the middle-aged gentleman's stunning features. He was perfectly groomed, too. The hand that held the elevator door was manicured, and I had no doubt the resort clothes he wore were expensive. I waited as Neely typed information into her phone. Domino was exploring the area around us until we moved again after a telltale whoosh indicated Neely's message was hurtling toward Charly's phone.

"Domino didn't seem to be bothered by him, but I'm too paranoid to make light of a chance encounter with anyone. Even a handsome, well-spoken, charmer with big, blue eyes. Maybe it was the ring on his hand," I said.

"It obviously wasn't a wedding ring, but maybe it's a flashy gift from a lady friend. This is the sort of place that attracts gigolos."

"You've spent more time with Hollywood types in places like this than I have, so I'll take your word for it. He was better dressed than I am, so I'm more likely to be a gold digger."

"Gigolos and gold diggers always show up dressed to kill, Miriam. I can take care of it if you're feeling underdressed. Did you pack any of the resort clothes that I bought you at Two?"

"No, that would have been a great idea. I thought we were here on the less fashionable business of snooping and that we were going to stay at the Schooner Inn." Neely glanced at her phone before tucking it back into a shoulder bag. When her hand came out, she held her wallet.

"I have a credit at the shops. Hang on. Let me see. Oh, yes, there's plenty. We've got time and money. Let's swing by, and get you something nice to wear."

"Neely, this has got to stop!"

"Why? I don't have a real daughter. I enjoy having a pretend one. Besides, I'm beholden to you for the insurance payout. And, I'm guessing that Nick Martinique isn't too old to appreciate a little attention from an attractive, well-dressed woman." She lifted her shades and raised her eyebrows a couple of times. "I'll do your makeup, and we'll fit you out to play femme fatale if need be."

I stopped, rendered speechless for a second time in less than an hour by the woman standing there. The wild gleam in her green eyes behind thick glasses was a perfect counterpart to the riotous salt and pepper curls that hung unrestrained below her shoulders. I leaned in and gave her a big hug.

"You know what? Let's save the shopping for tomorrow. I have a notion there's a better way to open a conversation with Nick Martinique. I'm going to dress down, not up—if they don't have a dress code at The Maiden Inn. In fact, all I need to do when we get back from the beach is change my shirt." I told her which shirt I had in mind, and what I'd seen on the Internet that made me think it might work better as an icebreaker than a tight skirt and décolletage.

"There's no dress code. The place is offbeat but a local favorite," Neely said.

"That's an excellent characterization of the pictures I saw. Most of the patrons were dressed for the beach."

"Yep. I'll bet casual and offbeat suits him to a T, don't you think?"

"You're right. Offbeat could also explain how someone hired an ex-convict and drug addict as a night manager."

Neely nodded in agreement with me and then dashed ahead as Domino and I hustled to catch up with her. My scheme was simple enough. If only I could take Domino along with us to dinner, but that seemed far-fetched.

"Hey, Neely, any chance they allow dogs in the outside dining area?"

"Ooh! That's brilliant, Miriam. Even better than wearing your Animal Rescue Walkathon t-shirt with Domino's picture on it! Let me give them a call and ask." A minute later, she gave me a thumbs up. I was elated until we turned the corner, and I glanced up at the man on the balcony.

"Don't look now, but Ricardo Cantinela is standing on his balcony. I'd like to believe he's hanging out there to catch the sunset. No binoculars like Jimmy Dunn at Dickens' Dune, but the alarms are going off in my head."

"How do you like that? Maybe he's infatuated with you, Miriam, but I don't like another coincidental sighting of the handsome fellow so soon any more than you do. I'm going to text Charly and ask her to sic Hank on him. Match my stride, will you?" She whipped out her phone and began snapping pictures of the beach and ocean, and then she turned and clicked away, taking several pictures of the resort.

"Did you get him?" I asked as she thumbed through the pictures on her phone.

"They're not great, but Charly or Hank can find someone to enhance them." I ran a little with Domino and then did a phony spin, positioning myself to check out the balcony again. Ricardo Cantinela was gone.

Where is he? I wondered. *Who is he?* This time, when Neely's phone issued that whoosh sound, I jumped out of my skin. The sound was barely audible above the pounding of the waves, but still loud enough to startle me.

"It's okay, Miriam. We're probably overreacting and should take Dickens' admonition seriously for now. *"Circumstances may accumulate so strongly even against an innocent man, that directed, sharpened, and pointed, they may slay him."*

"I hear you. I'm willing to admit that being confronted by a thug who turns up dead minutes later, may have me jumping to conclusions about an innocent man."

As a rosy pink appeared in the sky, I called Domino to me. She'd calmed down, but I didn't need to exhaust her. We weren't going to leave her in our suite to snooze. We had another man to meet who clearly wasn't always an innocent man. While he'd served his time for his drug-related misdeeds, I couldn't help but wonder if he had a hand in the murder of Allen Rogow.

10

Bah! Humbug!

"Bah!" said Scrooge, "Humbug."
—A Christmas Carol

∞

"NICK MARTINIQUE SPENT a few months at The Men's Colony for his third drug-related offense in two years. Not at the same time as Allen Rogow, but the following year. His stint did overlap with Leonard Cohen, although his police record doesn't tell us if they palled around together. Nick was a model citizen, completed treatment while he was in the facility, and they released him early."

"Let me clarify what you're saying, aloud, so Neely can hear it, okay, Charly? She may have questions."

"Sure."

"When Nick was sent to The Men's Colony, Leonard Cohen was there, and Allen Rogow had been released. Was that before Allen disappeared or after?" I asked Charly.

"After. I've been working on a timeline to track where Allen and each of his felonious associates were before and after he vanished. I'll send you a copy, so you'll have it to check against whatever story Nick Martinique gives you if I can get it done that fast. That's assuming he'll speak to you."

"A timeline to track who was in prison when would really be helpful, given the dubious company Allen kept." Neely bobbed her head up and down in enthusiastic support of my comment. "Mark Viceroy, Nick Martinique, and even Wendy Ballard all seem capable of killing him, if Leonard Cohen had it right, and he was murdered."

"Since we don't have a time of death for Allen, it's hard to give anyone an alibi—except Judith, of course, who was out of the area for the entire few days that Allen was in and around Dickens' Dune."

"Even though there wasn't a body on Dickens' Dune, the call to the police about finding Allen's dog tags must help narrow down the window of time in which a murder might have occurred," I suggested.

"True, but I haven't found anything yet that says the police had much to go on about who might have been in the area with him. Wendy and Nick used each other as an alibi, and Wendy claimed her car wasn't working and was in the shop. Nick backed her up on that, too."

"Did the police bother to check to see if her car really was in the shop for service?"

"Yes. On the face of it, she seems to have been telling the truth. It would have raised questions for me, though, that the garage was owned by one of Allen's Army buddies—Thomas Hilton—now deceased. Judith said she gave the police his name, along with those of Allen's other Army buddies, but their investigation was focused more on a missing person rather than a murdered one. Who knows if they even dug deep enough to discover that the owner of the garage was one of the men who might have been with Allen when that mishap occurred on Dickens' Dune?"

"Okay, that is interesting, Charly. I can understand the Army buddies closing ranks if one of them was involved in killing Allen. What I don't get is how Wendy Ballard figures into the picture."

"I like your plan for catching Nick off guard. Putting him at ease by appealing to his love of animals and taking Domino along to win him over might work. I reviewed the photos you sent, and you're right that he and the owners of The Maiden Inn have been active in their support of animal rescue efforts. It'll take some skill to keep him from bolting when you shift from small talk to the real reason for your visit, but if anyone can pull it off, you and Neely can. Even if he bolts, he might get back to you later once he calms down."

"If Nick Martinique has grown any wiser with age, he'll consider the possibility that the police might be looking into the matter again. Neely and I are easier to talk to than the cops," I said.

"I agree. Here's another point to work into the conversation if you need more leverage. Assuming Nick Martinique's not the killer, whoever did kill Allen might not be happy that Leonard has rekindled interest in the cold case. Nick needs to realize he's a loose end if he has any information about Allen Rogow's demise that he hasn't already shared with the police."

"That's sure true if Mark Viceroy is the culprit. He's

ruthless, given the carnage he and the other inmates caused while they were in prison at Calipatria." I got the shivers again just talking about him after reading about the Calipatria incident last night. It was another reason that I had so much trouble sleeping. "I can't believe he's still alive and a free man."

"He's still alive, although it's not clear for how long. Much of his last few months of incarceration were spent in the infirmary dealing with serious kidney problems. If Joe and Carl can't get a lead on his whereabouts from anyone in the veterans clubs they're visiting today, maybe someone at the VA dialysis center will recognize his name and can tell them where he's living."

"If he's that sick, he ought to be cooling his heels rather than stalking Nick Martinique or anyone else. Good luck getting the medical staff to answer questions about a patient," I said, sighing.

"They won't have to ask questions about anything in Mark Viceroy's medical record. Joe will get creative if need be. I've also sent the information to Midge."

"That's a great idea. Midge can work the rumor mill. After what went on at Calipatria, Mark Viceroy's reputation must precede him wherever he goes."

"I think so, too. Let's see what Midge can do with her connections to insiders who trust her," Charly added with what I sensed as hesitation in her voice as if she hadn't quite finished her sentence. When she didn't speak, I did.

"I'll review our conversation with Neely on our way to dinner," I said ready to get a move on.

"Speaking of people with connections, I've got news about your mystery man." My heart skipped a beat.

"Don't tell me, Ricardo Cantinela is a well-known con artist who bilks rich women out of their money." I tried to sound lighthearted, but Charly's tone had been sobering. "He's wasting his time if that's why he's introduced himself to me."

"That's not it," she responded. My heart skipped two beats. "Miriam, Ricardo Cantinela's connections aren't the romantic kind. He's in business with the mob. Before you panic, he's not a hired gun, he's a lawyer."

"Good grief! He's more likely to pass for a male model than a mob lawyer. Neely and I had him pegged as a gigolo." Neely, who was ready to go, had Domino on her leash and had her hand on the doorknob. She stopped and turned to face me.

"Apparently, he's a first-rate lawyer. Once I figured out who he was, I called Hank, who says there's a reason he's in town. The police picked up a suspect in Jimmy Dunn's murder. After the incidents at Shakespeare Cottage, our security people installed surveillance cameras like the ones Joe bought. One of them caught a picture of a guy striding across the golf course not far from where Jimmy Dunn met his end. Even though it wasn't a great shot, it was good enough to identify him when he tried to get on a plane at the San Luis Obispo Regional Airport yesterday. 'Lawyer' was the first word out of his mouth."

"Ricardo Cantinela didn't waste any time, did he?" I snapped.

"No, he did not. I'm sure he's working on some procedural angle to spring the man the police have in custody. A few images on a surveillance camera are circumstantial evidence at best. Unless they come up with something else, quickly, they're not going to be able to keep him locked up for long. Ricardo Cantinela's speedy arrival on the scene reassures me that Jimmy Dunn's movements were being tracked. Yours, too, Miriam. I don't believe it was an accident Cantinela showed up at the same resort and contacted you soon after you arrived."

"How worried should I be?"

"If they planned to kill you, Miriam, I doubt he would have bothered to introduce himself."

"He didn't apologize either after his dead associate scared the daylights out of me. What is going on?"

"I don't know, and neither does Hank, but we both agree no one is likely to mess with you now that Cantinela's involved. You can bet that the authorities are watching his every move."

"I guess that's good as long as I don't get caught in the crossfire while they play this cat and mouse game. I'm pretty sure I'm the mouse. This is the most gorgeous resort I've ever seen. It would be a shame to see it riddled with bullet holes—assuming I live to see it." Charly chuckled.

"Very funny. Go about your business," Charly snorted. "I'm trying to reassure you that our earlier conversation about Jimmy Dunn being a rogue elephant was on target."

"Rogue elephants have a way of trampling everything in their path. Thanks for the heads up about Cantinela."

I said goodbye to Charly and put away my phone. As we rode to the lobby, Neely and I chatted about the slick mob lawyer. "I hope he found the lie about my last name amusing. I'd rather have him laughing at me than angry enough to wring my neck."

"He didn't appear to be angry," Neely said. When the door opened, we scanned the corridor just in case he was waiting to bump into us again. "I don't see him, do you?"

"No," I replied, hustling into the lobby, still watchful. "Just because we can't see him, doesn't mean he doesn't have someone watching us."

I felt conspicuous and exposed as I crossed the lobby. As always, Domino drew the lion's share of the attention. Neely's car was waiting when we exited the lobby. Still, I didn't relax until we were on our way to The Maiden Inn.

"I never thought I'd say this, but chatting up a possible murder suspect seems like a lark compared to hanging out at a five-star resort with that blue-eyed devil lurking around," I said.

"Who wouldn't be anxious with a representative of Murder Incorporated putting the moves on them?" Neely asked.

"The Big Bad Wolf is trying to lure Little Red Riding Hood into his lair," I harrumphed. "Bah! Humbug!"

"Grandma's right here with you. He won't get a free pass from this grand old lady." I chortled at Neely's remark.

"We're wise to him now. He's a wolf in sheep's clothing even if he's not wearing one of your nightgowns." We both had a good laugh at that. Then I started at the beginning and tried to pass along in detail all the latest information from Charly.

"Nick Martinique has to be savvier now that he's all grown up. He was a baby back then. From what Judith told us, he was a doped-up dupe following Wendy Ballard around like her lap dog."

"Maybe the doped-up dupe needed drugs he couldn't pay for and lost it when Allen Rogow refused to give them to him."

"That could be," Neely agreed. "Raging killer drug fiend fits Wendy Ballard better than Nick Martinique from what Charly has learned about her criminal record. Allen had a rough go of it in Vietnam, but he made it back alive. Whoever killed him had to be someone close to him. I find it hard to believe either Nick or Wendy got the upper hand with him. My money's on Mark Viceroy or one of Allen's other Army buddies as his killer."

"Mark Viceroy gives me the shivers. He stands out among Allen's so-called friends as the most vicious. Desperation can trump friendship, can't it? That's what I keep telling myself when it comes to understanding how Pete managed to get me into a situation that involves a personal introduction from a mob lawyer. One to whom I lied, by the way."

"I'm sure he found it funny. He lied, too, when he pretended that he didn't know who we were."

Neely patted my arm and then switched on her turn signal. We had no problem spotting The Maiden Inn. Finding a parking place was a breeze too. Much to my surprise, Nick Martinique wasn't hard to find either. While we waited at the entrance to the outdoor seating area, I elbowed Neely.

"Domino's working her magic. Look who has a smile on his face." Nick Martinique wore a brightly colored aloha shirt, shorts, and sandals. He hadn't changed much from the photo I'd found. He was a little older, and his hair was wispier as the breeze blew through it. The smile on his face faded as his eyes moved from Domino to us.

"Follow me, and I'll show you to your table, Ms. Webster." I'd started to do just that until he addressed me by name. No introductions required.

"Thanks, Mr. Martinique." When we reached our table, Domino went to work on him. He obviously couldn't resist the sweet girl who wiggled and whipped his leg with her tail. It was a cool night, so there weren't many of us seated on the large patio. Strings of tiny lights above us flickered as air blowing in from offshore caused them to sway ever so slightly. Given the chill in the air, I was grateful the heaters had been turned on. Although, not all the chilliness had anything to do with the ocean breeze. Once we were seated and a server took our drink orders, Nick pulled up a seat and joined us.

"What is it you want, Ms. Conrad? Where are the rest of your Grand Old Lady Detectives? You sure hit it big when you helped bust a smuggling ring right in your own backyard."

"It's Neely, please, Nick. I'd prefer to be on a first-name basis if that's okay with you." Nick shrugged. She continued. "Since you seem tuned in on new developments in the area on the crime front, you must have heard about Leonard Cohen's claims that someone murdered an old friend of yours."

"I have. Some punk police officer, who looked to be about twelve years old, came by and asked me about it." Neely and I glanced at each other, trying to hide our surprise that the police were making inquiries. Domino yawned and then leaned her head against Nick's leg. He reached down and rubbed her soft ears, and his body language changed as he instantly relaxed.

"What did you tell him?" I asked.

"That it all happened a long time ago and my memory sucks. Methamphetamine does a number on your body and your mind. I'm lucky I can remember my own name." He was getting riled up again and stopped petting Domino. She pawed at his arm and smiled. "She's your secret weapon, huh?"

"I'm lucky to have her in my life, Nick." He made eye contact, and a flicker of something like recognition passed through them.

"One of the stories mentioned you were a recent widow. I'm sorry for your loss." Before he could say anything else, our drinks arrived.

"Do you two like fresh seafood? I'd recommend the barramundi with citrus salsa. You can't go wrong with anything the chef has on the menu, but the fish is excellent. I never ate so well until I started this job."

"The barramundi sounds wonderful."

"To me, too," Neely added.

"Can Domino eat chicken?" Nick asked.

"Sure. She loves it."

"Cindy, will you tell the chef to send out a plain broiled chicken breast for the pooch, please?" Cindy smiled, and a dimple appeared in our server's little round face.

"Of course, I will. What a beautiful dog. So well-behaved, too." As soon as Cindy was out of earshot, I decided to press Nick for his help.

"Nick, was Leonard Cohen telling the truth? Did someone kill Allen Rogow?" He looked side to side, the lights glinted off the lenses of his glasses as he turned his head.

11

Unexpected Tears

"We need never be ashamed of our tears."
—Great Expectations

∞

"WHEN I SAID my memory sucks, I was telling the truth. Something happened that night, but I honestly can't tell you what."

"You were there—on Dickens' Dune?"

"Yes. I didn't want to go, but Wendy insisted. Allen was her friend, not mine, although she was convinced it was love, not friendship. He suddenly broke it off with her, said he was done getting high and was going to turn his life around. Wendy was a miserable wreck for days. I tried to get her to calm down, and then Mark dropped by armed with comfort in pill form." When Nick spoke again, it was barely above a whisper.

"That guy was whacked even when he wasn't high or drunk. He got a little stoned, and let it slip that he and several guys he served with in Vietnam, were going camping with Allen near the Nipomo Dunes. After he left, Wendy got it into her head that if she could only talk to

Allen, she could change his mind about going back to his wife."

I almost did a spit take hearing Nick confirm that Allen had hoped to reconcile with Judith even though they were divorced. I had to bite my tongue to keep myself from interrupting him with a dozen questions. I'm glad I restrained myself because Nick was suddenly overcome by emotion. Tears streaming down the leathered cheeks of the seemingly jaded man stunned me.

"Sorry, about the tears. Yesterday was my sister's birthday. She would have been sixty-two if she hadn't died from an overdose."

"Sister?" We asked in tandem.

"Yes, I assumed you'd already figured that out. Wendy and I were adopted, so we have different last names, but we had the same birth mother and never lost touch. As soon as I turned eighteen, I moved in with Wendy. I knew she was in trouble with drugs. I swore I wouldn't let her end up like our mother, but I failed. Instead of getting her clean and sober after I moved in, I joined the party."

Then the unexpected tears returned. Nick hung his head and sobbed quietly. Domino put both paws on his leg, trying to get his attention. He dried his eyes on the napkin at the table, and then patted Domino's head.

"It's okay, girl. I'm embarrassed about the tears, and I don't want you to take what I'm about to say the wrong way. We would have been better off if Mark Viceroy had died or disappeared that night instead of Allen Rogow."

"We never need to be ashamed of our tears," Neely said. "Or any display of honest emotions, for that matter. Mark Viceroy is still alive, so it's obvious you didn't act on your anger toward him."

"Maybe Wendy would have been better off if I had. He supplied us both with drugs, and I'm sure he's the one who gave her the dose that killed her—whether she wanted it or not. When she died, I couldn't stand being around here for another minute."

"When you say he supplied her with drugs, I take it you mean he was a dealer, not Allen Rogow."

"Yes. Allen had feelings for her and refused to sell or give her drugs, and he told her to get back into treatment. Wendy thought he was in love with her, but I think he saw her more like a sister. Mark, on the other hand, had his eye on her as a girlfriend. Mark was happy when Allen told us he was moving out. I'm sure that jerk would gladly have sold drugs to his own sister. Maybe that's because he wanted to make it big. Mark was more committed to the drug business than Allen, with ambitions to be a kingpin." My mind was racing wondering how Mark's ambitions for his relationship with Wendy and his career as a dealer might have been related to whatever happened to Allen.

"So, what do you remember? Anything about what happened that night on Dickens' Dune?"

"Wendy and I had started partying before we got there. It wasn't that far to Dickens' Dune from our apartment in San Luis Obispo, but don't ask me how my sister drove that far or found her way to Dickens' Dune if she was as wasted as I was. I remember laughing hysterically while trying to hike in that condition as it was getting dark. We slipped and slid, and I hit the ground hard at one point. Wendy had a good laugh at me, but when she did the same thing, and I laughed at her, she smacked me. I never have been able to take a punch. The last thing I remember clearly is walking into an old bunker during a disagreement between Mark and Allen."

"What about?" I asked.

"Allen was ticked that Mark was using the old bunker to sell drugs to high school kids, but they were also arguing about money."

"Drug money?"

"Probably. There were a couple of thugs in the bunker I'd never seen before, so maybe Mark or Allen owed them money. When Mark and Allen realized Wendy and I had joined the party, they shut up. Mark grabbed Wendy and tried to kiss her. She took a swing at him, and he hit her. Like the idiot that I was, I charged him, fists flying, and took it on the chin, and the lights went out. When I came to, the sun was coming up, and the others were gone. Wendy was shaking me and telling me to wake up so we could go home."

"You really can't take a punch if you were out that long," Neely said in a skeptical tone. Nick shrugged.

"Maybe I would have passed out even if Mark hadn't punched me. Or he could have hit me again as I fell. My face was a mess the next day. I told you that we were wasted, and I don't remember much."

"Your memory is better than you said. Did you tell the police about any of this?" Neely asked in a low voice. There wasn't anyone seated nearby, but Nick appeared to be getting antsy.

"No. Wendy wouldn't let me. She said if we talked to the police, we'd all get arrested for drugs and assault and who knew what else? So, I kept my mouth shut. I always figured something bad must have happened because Mark never asked us to pay a cent for drugs after that. According to my sister, Mark had moved up the food chain and could take a cut of the drugs he sold."

"Did she say what happened to Allen?" I asked, wondering if Mark had moved up by getting rid of Allen if he perceived him to be a competitor.

"No, but it seemed obvious to me that Mark or those thugs had killed Allen and ditched the body somewhere. When the police stopped by our apartment to ask about Allen's whereabouts, we said we had no idea, which was true for me anyway. Then, when they asked where we'd been the night before, we lied and said we'd been stuck at home because Wendy's car had broken down on us."

"Yeah, we heard Wendy told the police her car was in the shop." Nick looked hard at me. His eyes were still a little red from crying which undermined the set of his jaw. "Look, I'm not going to turn you in, although I will encourage you to contact a detective friend of ours and tell him everything you've told us." I pulled out a pen and wrote Hank's name and phone number on a cocktail napkin.

"I'll think about it," he said when I slid the napkin across the table. Then he picked up where he'd left off. "When we got home, it was still early. Mark had let himself into our apartment and was waiting for us. It was his idea to have a friend pick up the car and take it to his shop, and then tell anyone who asked about where we'd been the night before that we were stranded at home because the car had conked out on us. I was suspicious of his motives, but Wendy was so grateful, she threw her arms around his neck. It was as if he'd never hit her and was doing her a favor instead of making sure a couple of druggies didn't let something slip. I wanted to throttle him, but I wasn't going to take him on again."

Our server showed up with our meals, and he shut up. Nick placed the paper plate with Domino's treat on it on the patio floor in front of her. Domino looked at me as if it was too good to be true.

"Aren't you lucky? Nick had that made especially for you." She nuzzled his hand and then gulped down the chicken before Neely or I had even taken a bite. Nick smiled and shook his head.

"I'd love to have a girl like her in my life. She knows how to eat, doesn't she?"

"She sure does. Can you have a dog where you're living?" I asked.

"Yes, but I'd probably have to go all the way to San Francisco or LA to find a beauty like Domino." He pushed back his chair as if he was going to stand up. "Enjoy your meal. Dessert's on me if you have room for it."

"We know how to eat, too, Nick," Neely said and winked at him.

"I'll bet you do. Try the chef's Crème Brûlée; you won't be disappointed." Then he let out a sigh so big it's as if his body deflated right before my eyes. "I was too messed up to think straight back then. To be honest, when Wendy overdosed, I'd started to use drugs again after getting myself clean at The Men's Colony. I figured it was only a matter of time before I ended up like her—accidentally or on purpose—if I got desperate enough to go back to Mark Viceroy as my source. Years later, when I heard that he was mixed up in that incident at Calipatria, I figured he'd die in prison. It finally felt safe to return. He's out now, though, isn't he?"

"Yes," I replied. "Which is another reason to tell Hank Miller everything you know about Mark Viceroy and what went on at Dickens' Dune."

"I might as well. What have I got to lose?" I tried not to think about that as he gave Domino a last hug. He'd made his share of mistakes, but he'd paid dearly for them.

"That was revealing," Neely said as he walked away. "He seemed sincere, didn't he?"

"Yes, but I couldn't help feeling he knows more than he's willing to say."

"What makes you say that?"

"His memory of what went on at Dickens' Dune was too good at times to be as bad as he claimed it was at other times. I think that's a convenient way to avoid laying it all out on the table."

"I suppose that's possible if he's still afraid that he'll go to jail if he goes to the police. At his age, I'm sure he doesn't want to spend his golden years in lockup. Let's hope he decides to sit down with Hank. Unless he killed Allen Rogow or had a hand in burying the body, it's too late to charge him for any lesser crimes he and his sister committed that night."

"Wendy Ballard sure sounded like she was mad enough to kill someone. Maybe she murdered Allen and Nick's protecting her even though she's dead," I suggested.

"He sure is carrying a load of guilt about letting her down while she was alive. In his mind, outing her as a murderer might feel like he's doing it again."

"Or he's scared to death that Mark Viceroy will get revenge if he goes to the authorities." I paused for a second, trying to figure out what was nagging me about another issue—the argument about money. The image of Pete with his hand out to Jimmy Dunn floated into my weary brain. "If Mark Viceroy wanted to make it big in the drug business, wouldn't he have had to come up with lots of cash? They're not going to hand over a load of drugs on credit, are they?"

"I've never seen drug buys on credit in any of the movies I've watched. Otherwise, I'm not all that well versed in how drug deals work. I could ask a couple of my old friends in Hollywood about how their connections worked, although I don't believe any of them ever approached kingpin status."

"No! All we need is to attract attention from members of the drug cartel in addition to mobsters and psycho ex-convicts if Mark Viceroy has heard that a gang of old people are asking questions about him."

"Okay, okay! Maybe we ought to start reading more in the True Crime genre. I gather the point you're making is that the money he and Allen were arguing about wasn't chicken feed."

"Right, I'm talking about big bucks, not chump change!"

"I'm going to call Charly and bring her up to speed," Neely said. "I'm curious about what the money argument was about, too. I'll see if she's had a chance to snoop into Mark Viceroy's finances. Maybe the place to start is to figure out how he's making ends meet now that the State of California is no longer paying for his upkeep."

"That's a very good place to start. If Wendy was right that he'd moved up the ranks as a drug dealer, his success was short-lived before his arrest. Even though he escaped, hiding out from the law all those years must have put a crimp in his criminal career," I argued.

"Maybe not. Dealing in illegal drugs could have been the way he survived while he was underground. If he squirreled away cash before he was finally caught and sent to Calipatria, that could be what he's using now."

"Ask Charly about the money, and let her figure it out. She has more experience than the two of us combined when it comes to thinking like a criminal." Neely didn't sound the least bit tired when she laughed at the idea of telling Charly what I'd said.

When we got back to the hotel later, I was too exhausted to worry about another encounter with Ricardo Cantinela. I dragged myself through the lobby to the elevator without even looking around. As it turned out, that would have been pointless.

"Hello! How fortunate to run into the two most attractive females I've seen all day," Ricardo Cantinela said the moment the elevator doors slid open. He was looking at Domino as he spoke so I couldn't be sure to whom he was referring.

"Thanks, Attorney Cantinela," Neely responded. "You're not half-bad to look at, either."

I had to bite my tongue to keep from laughing out loud at the expression of surprise on the man's face. I couldn't tell what had shocked him, Neely's cheeky comment about his looks or addressing him as an attorney.

He had two grim-faced bodyguards with him. When

Ricardo Cantinela broke into a smile, they snickered, and I had a good laugh, too. What a strange day—unexpected tears followed by unexpected laughter. What could possibly happen next?

12

Friends with Chocolate

"There is nothing better than a friend, unless it is a friend with chocolate."

—Charles Dickens

∞

"THAT'S ROOM SERVICE. I need coffee so, I already ordered breakfast." Neely hollered when there was a knock on the door the next morning. "Tell the server to set it up for us on the veranda unless you're worried the hitmen in your life are early risers."

"Ha-ha! Very funny. You don't need coffee—you're already wide awake." Domino, who had been chowing down in the kitchen, ran for the door when she heard that knock. She woofed and spun around.

"You're wound up too? Am I the only one who's pooped this morning?" I opened the door still watching Domino's silliness.

"Come on in and set up on the lanai, please."

"Set up what where?" Joe asked as he stepped into the room, carrying an enormous bouquet of flowers. Carl strode into the room behind him, with a huge box of chocolates.

"What are you doing here?" I asked.

"That's no way to welcome friends—especially friends bearing chocolate." Carl held the box up to his ear and rattled it. "I assume it's candy—there's nothing ticking, and I smell chocolate."

"You didn't buy it?" Neely asked as she wandered into the sitting area of our suite.

"No. We rode up on the elevator with a delivery guy. When we realized we were all going to the same place, we said we'd make sure you got it." Carl's eyes wandered around the suite and then settled on the gorgeous view. "We gave him a nice tip, too, and told him to put it on your tab."

"To which he responded, 'no can do.' When I asked what that meant, he assured us the sender had already taken care of it. Has Hank kicked it up a notch?" Joe asked as he took the flowers to the kitchen, and stood them upright in the sink.

"There's a new man in Miriam's life. He's loaded—probably in more than one sense of the word," Neely snickered.

"Go ahead and laugh. You'll miss me when I'm gone!" I quipped as Carl and Joe stood there waiting for an explanation.

"The punster in our midst means loaded as in packing heat as well as rolling in dough."

"Duh," Carl responded. "What I want to know is why a guy like that has taken a sudden interest in you?" I was trying to figure out how to respond when there was another knock on the door.

"Room service!"

"Thank goodness the coffee has arrived. Don't ask me to share. I need a whole pot if I'm going to catch up with the rest of you." This time, I did what I should have done earlier—used the peephole to make sure it really was someone from room service delivering our breakfast.

"Yay, coffee! Come on in, please. Can you roll that out to the veranda?"

"Of course—my pleasure." In minutes our breakfast was set up, and the young man from room service even poured me a cup of coffee. "Will there be anything else?"

"That'll do it," Neely replied as she signed the ticket. She must have added a nice tip because the grin on his face widened when he took it from her. After he was gone, I'd barely had a sip of coffee when Carl and Joe demanded to know what was going on. I hesitated for a minute, wondering if we could be overheard while we sat on the large balcony that ran the length of the two-bedroom suite.

"Oh, what the heck?" I muttered. "My life is an open book these days—to everyone but me, anyway." It didn't take long to fill them in about Ricardo Cantinela. In fact, there was surprisingly little to say.

"Charly mentioned that they'd picked up someone suspected of killing Jimmy Dunn and that he'd lawyered up—courtesy of the Ohio mob. She neglected to add the best part, though. Does Hank know he's got a rival for your affections?" Carl asked. The snickering had begun again, but I wasn't sure Carl's question was so funny.

"Hank can hold his own with a slick lawyer dude any day," Joe added as he helped himself to a strip of bacon from a small plate sitting on the cart.

"What brings you here so bright and early?" I asked as I passed the plate to Carl and then sat down to eat my breakfast.

"We wanted to see how the other half lives," Carl quipped. "This makes our hotel room look like a dump."

"I don't believe you for a second," Neely snapped. "What's up?"

"Charly thought we should compare notes—share what we learned from our round of visits yesterday. She said you might have news for us, too, if your conversation with Nick Martinique went well last night."

"Did you find him at The Maiden Inn?" Joe asked.

"We did," Neely replied. "I must have spoken to Charly after you did because I told her about our dinner conversation with Nick Martinique. He had plenty to say, although Miriam doesn't believe he told us the whole story about what happened at Dickens' Dune. He and Wendy Ballard, who, as it turns out, is his sister, were there the night we figure things went bad for Allen."

"His sister?" Carl asked.

"They were there—at Dickens' Dune?" Joe added as he made himself comfortable on a nearby chaise. I nodded, and then Neely and I filled them in on the information we'd picked up from Nick Martinique, trying to hit the important points.

"I hope he takes your advice about calling Hank—pronto! We talked to one of the guards who was working at The Men's Colony when Allen Rogow and Leonard Cohen were inmates."

"How'd you manage to do that?" I asked.

"We hung around at lunchtime until a couple of the oldest-looking guards came out. Then we followed them to a local diner, and asked if we could buy them lunch in exchange for stories about their experiences on the inside."

"They bought that?" Neely asked.

"Yeah, it worked great! Even when we told them we were interested in stories about a guy we knew who's dead now."

"Joe had to order a round of pie to sweeten the deal." I rolled my eyes at more punny humor and poured myself another cup of coffee.

"Only one of the two men had been at the facility long enough to remember Allen Rogow—a war hero with a drug problem was how our lunch partner, Skip, remembered him," Joe said. Carl jumped in at that point.

"As soon as Joe brought up Allen's name, he asked us if Allen was murdered after he got out of prison. We told him that's what we were trying to find out. He suggested we check out a *'whack-job'* by the name of Mark Viceroy who came to visit Allen more than once. Shortly before Allen was released, he and his buddy, Mark, got into it."

"As in a verbal disagreement, or were punches thrown?" Neely asked.

"Mark Viceroy threw a punch, but Allen dodged it. The guards in the room went into action and got Mark under control. They escorted him out of there, although it took two of them to do it."

"They should have called the local police and held him there until they picked him up." Neely shook her head.

"If that punch had landed, they probably could have

charged him with assault and battery and made it stick," Carl said.

"That could have been a forewarning of things to come, huh?" I asked. Neely nodded as I asked another question. "Did Skip tell you about Mark Viceroy's role in a disastrous escape attempt from Calipatria? That would have earned him the whack-job label."

"Yes, but Skip says he'd nailed the guy as a ticking time bomb long before that," Joe said. "He tried to get them to ban Mark Viceroy as a visitor before he took that swing at Allen. Mark had turned up at the facility angry, cursing, and making rude remarks about the guards on duty and other visitors."

"And high as a kite, according to Skip," Carl added.

"Yep. They always searched him to make sure he wasn't bringing drugs into the facility to pass along to Allen Rogow, or the other guy he visited once or twice. They never found anything on him." Neely and I instantly reacted to the "other guy" part of Joe's comment.

"Whoa—wait! Time out," I said using both hands to make the T-sign.

"The other guy, who?" Neely asked.

"Didn't I already say something about that?"

"No!" Even Carl joined in responding to Joe's question.

"Senior moment, sorry. Mark Viceroy also visited Leonard Cohen. After one of those visits, Leonard was as pale as a ghost when he left the visitors' room."

"Did Skip say why?" The moment the question was out of my mouth, I realized it was a stupid one. Joe would have been eager to share that information if the prison guard had given it to him.

"He didn't know, but Leonard made sure Mark was never allowed to visit him again."

"If he was that scared, it's easier to understand why he didn't come forward about Allen's murder until he was on his deathbed," Neely commented. "I would have loved to have been a fly on the wall or somewhere close enough to hear what passed between them."

"A cheer must have gone up when Mark Viceroy ended up behind bars at Calipatria—once they put him away for a long time in maximum security," I added.

"That's the truth. We had no trouble finding old guys in the SLO veterans organizations who knew who he was," Joe said.

"Sorry to interrupt, but what are slow veterans organizations?" I asked.

"S-L-O—as in short for San Luis Obispo," Carl replied. "They use nicknames around here too."

"Okay, thanks. Please go on, will you? I take it that Mark wasn't well-behaved among his fellow vets, either." Carl and Joe both nodded in response to the conclusion I'd reached.

"Sad, but true. They had their share of troubled vets, but Mark was ready to fight once he had a few drinks in him. Nasty if he lost a penny ante poker game. They called the cops on him at a couple of the places we visited to get him to leave, but he was always long gone by the time the cops arrived," Carl said. Joe spoke up next.

"This old guy, Ernie, who served in Vietnam, too, told us he was disgusted by Mark Viceroy's behavior. Ernie was mostly upset that Mark was trolling the place and peddling drugs. He admitted he'd called the cops and wasn't surprised that Mark left in such a hurry because he must have had drugs on him or in his car."

"That makes sense," I said. "Has he shown up since he was released a year ago?"

"He hasn't been seen at the places we visited—including several of the bars closest to the veteran's halls. Charly probably told you that his kidneys are wrecked, so it sounds like his drinking days are over," Carl said.

"Yeah, she told us the place he's most likely to visit these days is a VA dialysis unit," Neely commented. Then Joe spoke in an excited tone.

"Yes, and rumor has it that he shows up three times per week at the same time and place. We're planning a stakeout for this afternoon. He's there for two or three hours, and when he leaves, we'll follow him home. After we have an address for him, we'll call Charly and give it to her. She's hoping she can find out more about how he's paying for things like rent these days."

"How will you know it's him?" I asked.

"Charly sent us a copy of a picture she found with the California DMV. They issued him a new driver's license not long after he was released from prison last year."

"Doesn't that have an address on it?"

"Yes, but it was issued while he was still staying at a halfway house in Indio, not too far from Calipatria. Charly says he left there a few months ago, without leaving a forwarding address."

"Doesn't he have a parole officer he has to report to?" Neely asked.

"He does, and if we can't locate Mark Viceroy, we'll

try to get an appointment to see if his parole officer will tell us where we can find him," Carl replied. "If he even agrees to meet with us, I doubt he'll say much."

"I'll bet there's no employer information either or Charly would have found him like she did Nick." I was becoming frustrated at how elusive Mark Viceroy seemed to be.

"As sick as he is, who would hire him?" Neely asked.

"Now that Charly knows how bad his health was while he was in prison, she suspects he might be receiving disability benefits from the VA," Carl said. "She's looking into it."

"That would sure answer the question about how he's living now that he's out of prison. Miriam and I had cooked up a scenario speculating that he's living off money that he hid before he was sent to Calipatria."

"Even if he is on disability, there's still something strange going on with money," I insisted. I went back over parts of the conversation we'd had with Nick Martinique about the fight over money he overheard between Allen and Mark. "How about this? If Allen and Leonard knew each other before they went to prison, Allen could have given money to Leonard and he lost it. If the money belonged to Mark, too, he could have visited Leonard and tried to terrorize him into giving it back. Maybe when that didn't work, Mark blamed Allen and got into that argument in which he took a swing at Allen before the guards intervened," I suggested.

"Yeah, that would make sense if they argued about it again, and Mark lost control at Dickens' Dune. Mark may have settled the matter once and for all." Joe pretended to fire an imaginary gun.

"Judith made it sound like they met when they were both inmates at The Men's Colony. They both had a history of drug problems. What if they met in rehab or in an AA meeting?" Neely argued.

"Let's call Judith and see if Allen went for treatment anywhere before he was sent to The Men's Colony. He and Leonard could have crossed paths even if Allen didn't stay in treatment for long."

"That's a good idea. I say we also ask Charly to search their case files. There ought to be reports about previous efforts to seek treatment in the affidavits filed before their presentencing hearings. That's where their history of drug problems, and any efforts they already made to deal with them, would have been presented in some detail. Judith has already said Allen kept secrets from her, which would explain why she was under the impression they met while they were inmates at The Men's Colony."

"Okay, Neely, let's finish breakfast. Then you call Charly, and I'll call Judith."

"And I'll make sure the chocolate's good enough for the two of you." Neely and I had almost finished eating, and Joe had passed the box of chocolates to Carl when Neely's phone rang.

13

More Surprises

"Surprises, like misfortunes, seldom come alone."
—Charles Dickens

∞

"HI, MIDGE! HOW are you?" In the next instant, Neely was up on her feet. "Give me the address." She jotted down the address. "We weren't too far from there last night. We'll be there in ten or fifteen minutes—tops. Have you called Charly?"

The moment I heard Neely ask Midge for an address, I was on my feet. I scooped up dishes and cups and piled them onto the room service cart. By the time Neely asked Midge if she'd called Charly, I was rolling the cart through the suite to the hallway.

"Tell her we're on our way," I said as I grabbed Domino's leash, and slipped on my shoes.

"The Angels are on their way, too," Carl said as he towered over Neely and copied the address she'd written down. Neely passed along the message to Midge that we were all on our way and ended the call.

"On the way where? Why?"

"To a hotel just up the road, Joe," Carl replied, still looking at that address Midge had given Neely. "Neely will have to tell us why on the way to our cars."

"I don't have the details, but Midge and Marty followed Leonard Cohen's nurse—Elizabeth Stockton—here from Santa Barbara. I heard Marty telling Midge to make sure we know that she's a crook. She insisted that you bring Domino and that we call Charly."

"Why call Charly?" I asked.

"In case there's a Deputy Devers in this jurisdiction, and we get into a dodgy situation with the law. Midge and Marty are in Elizabeth Stockton's hotel room, and it's been trashed. She's gone, and they're going to call the police, but they want us to see something before the police arrive and declare it a crime scene."

When we got to the elevator, we didn't have to wait. I hit the button and the door slid open. Neely and Carl had called ahead for valet service, so both cars were at the curb by the time we bolted from the lobby. I called Charly and gave her a heads-up in case Midge needed help dealing with the San Luis Obispo police. Eight minutes later, we pulled into the hotel parking lot, and Marty waved us down before we could go inside to the check-in desk.

"This way," she said, and we followed her around the outside of the main building to a public pathway that led to the beach. Soon, Marty made a quick right turn, and we were on a slatted wooden walkway that ran in front of a row of beachfront cottages. Calling the tiny detached buildings cottages was a stretch. They weren't much bigger than garden sheds or beach cabanas. We dashed after Marty with the walkway clattering and squeaking underfoot until we reached the last cottage. The door was ajar, and Midge stood just inside the doorway.

"When you said trashed, you meant it!" Neely exclaimed. The room had been thoroughly and completely searched. Drawers were emptied, the chests and nightstands were overturned. The mattress was on the floor, and the bed upended. Someone had slashed the mattress, pillows, and chair cushions.

"Yeah, whoever did this must have been convinced Elizabeth Stockton had something important hidden in here. The police are on their way. This is what I wanted you to see before they arrive and close off access to this area. Didn't you mention that you saw a lightning symbol on the wall of the bunker?"

"Yes, I think that's what it was—in among other graffiti scrawled on the wall in there."

"Did it look anything like that?" she asked and pointed to some pieces of paper lying on the floor near an overturned wastebasket. Before it had been torn into four pieces, a bolt of lightning inside an oddly shaped border appeared to have been sketched onto a slip of paper torn from a hotel memo pad.

"There's definitely a resemblance, although the version I saw was even more crudely drawn—carved or scratched into the wall of the bunker near the floor."

"That looks to me like an emblem used to designate the infantry division Allen and his soldier buddies were attached to in Vietnam."

"What's it doing in here?" I asked.

"If you can find Elizabeth Stockton, ask her." Then Midge took us to the end of the slatted wooden walkway.

In the sand, just inches from where the walkway ended, was what looked like a drop of blood and footprints—two sets.

"Marty and I tried to catch up with Elizabeth and whoever ransacked her room. We followed the footprints up the beach to the boardwalk and gave up. I'm sure one set belongs to Elizabeth. Even though we lost the trail once we got to the boardwalk, I hoped Domino might have better luck. That's another reason I wanted you to get here ahead of the police." We all paused to listen to the wailing of police sirens. Midge continued, speaking with more urgency.

"Go now. Take Marty with you because she's seen Elizabeth Stockton. I need to stay here and try to convince the police the woman who occupied this room could be in danger. You know how police can be about a missing person—especially if we're dealing with a police officer like Devers. Getting them to act might take some time and effort."

"If what they see in that room isn't enough to make them worry about the occupant, show them the blood." Neely rolled her eyes.

"I'm not going to leave you here alone," Marty argued.

"The police will come barreling in here any minute, now. Besides, I'm not alone. Joe and Carl will stay with me, won't you guys?"

"For a while," Joe replied. "We have an appointment we can't afford to miss." If Joe had more to say, it didn't matter because Carl cut him off.

"That's not until three." Then, he turned to us.

"Listen to Midge and get out of here," Carl insisted.

"The sooner you put Domino to work, the better chance she has of tracking the woman who may have left here against her will." Domino was sniffing the walkway. Then she pawed at it and made digging motions.

"Look, Marty," Neely said, pointing at Domino. "Maybe she's already picked up something. I don't see a trace of blood, but Domino must be able to detect drops that fell through the slatted wooden walkway to the sand beneath it."

"I'll tell the police to check the area under this section of the walkway if I can get them to do it. Take this with you." Midge handed me a mailing envelope as she spoke to us about its contents. "I peeked inside, and a scarf is in there. The charge nurse told us it belongs to Elizabeth. If her scent is on it and Domino stalls out when you get to the boardwalk, it could help. Marty can explain how we got it."

At that point, we left in a hurry. The sirens were loud enough that the police had to be in front of the hotel by now. I assumed one of the officers would speak to whoever was at the front desk, but Midge could be right that others would head directly to the tiny cottage.

Domino eagerly followed the trail of footsteps. At one point, she stopped and whined before digging at the sand again. When I gave her leash a little tug, she continued toward the boardwalk. We were all breathing heavily as we tried to keep up with her. In between huffs and puffs, Marty gave us the scoop about Elizabeth Stockton as we hustled as fast as we could through the sand.

"We went to the hospital yesterday, expecting to have a chat with Elizabeth Stockton. One of Midge's friends who books appointments for the nursing staff put us on Elizabeth Stockton's calendar. Before she did that, she gave Midge an earful about Leonard Cohen. Apparently, he was more notorious than we realized. Especially in Santa Barbara, where he recruited many of the people he scammed. When he was admitted to the hospital by hospice, it created quite a stir."

"They have a long memory since his scamming days ended decades ago," I said and then paused before I continued. "Never mind, you don't have to tell me how long trouble can follow you after someone in your life has made stupid financial decisions."

"I couldn't have said it better myself," Neely added, giving me a reassuring pat on the back.

"Apparently, we just missed Elizabeth Stockton. According to the charge nurse, she stopped long enough to say she was late for an appointment, and in such a rush that she left that package sitting on the counter. Midge explained that Elizabeth's appointment was with us, so maybe she'd misunderstood and was on her way to meet us at our hotel."

"How'd you end up with the package?"

"She handed it to us in case Elizabeth had intended to take it with her to our meeting. Then she reassured us not to blame ourselves about the mix-up. Elizabeth had been preoccupied lately, and ours wasn't the first appointment she'd goofed up. The charge nurse sounded a little ticked but quickly apologized. 'Elizabeth has taken a few sick days, so maybe she's dealing with a health issue.' When I asked if she seemed ill before she left, she said no. In fact, she claimed she was more upbeat than she'd appeared to be in several weeks."

"How did you find out she was here?"

"Midge knew Elizabeth wasn't on her way to meet with us at our hotel or anywhere else. We had her home address, and we took a chance that she'd gone there. We hoped we could deliver that package to her and use it to start a conversation. Elizabeth didn't answer her door, and there was no car in the carport, so we went back to Midge's car. After almost an hour, we were about to leave when she suddenly appeared. Elizabeth parked under the carport and practically ran into her house. She was in such a hurry, we waited to see if someone was after her."

Marty hadn't finished her story, but she abruptly quit speaking as we reached the boardwalk. I let Domino check out the area. Marty must have thought she needed a little help and slid the scarf out of the envelope. It was neatly rolled up. As she unfurled the scarf, a tiny key on a chain tumbled to the ground.

While I bent down to pick up the key on its chain, Domino sniffed the envelope and scarf. Then she sniffed the boardwalk and started moving again, pulling me with her. She walked away from the beach and toward the street lined with shops and parking meters. Marty held the envelope for me so I could slip the key back into it.

"What do you want to bet Elizabeth intended to bring that key with her wherever she was headed?" Neely commented.

"Obviously, she was headed here," Marty responded. "We didn't even have a chance to get out of our car before Elizabeth Stockton was back carrying a suitcase. When she left, we followed her until she checked into the hotel here last night. We parked on a side street, and followed her to see what room she was in."

"I don't suppose you saw anyone else following her last night or waiting for her when she arrived?" Neely asked.

"No, but we could have missed it if someone was keeping an eye on her. We weren't the only people on the beach last night. The boardwalk was still all lit up, and there was still lots of action at the eateries and carnival rides."

"How could someone else have tracked her here unless they followed her, too?" I asked.

"Devers would blame us," Marty responded. "Elizabeth could have called someone before she left her office or once she arrived here. Our first impression was that she was on the run. Given what her colleague at the nurse's station told us about Elizabeth's upbeat mood, maybe she was just in a hurry to get here to keep a rendezvous she set up yesterday."

"That's possible," Neely said. "By the looks of her room, the rendezvous didn't go so well."

"Maybe she was supposed to bring that key with her," I mumbled. "What time was it the last time you saw her?"

"We checked into our hotel room a little before nine. We'd hung around, walking back and forth along the beach for well over an hour in case she had a dinner date. When she had pizza delivered to her door, we figured she was settled in for the night. We left soon after the delivery guy did, which I'd say was eight-thirty."

We came to a stop when we reached the point at which the boardwalk ended at a set of cement steps. At the top of the steps, we found ourselves at a crisscross of sidewalks. One set, to our right and left, ran parallel to stores and hotels on the beachside. Another ran straight ahead to the street and intersected with sidewalks that ran along the street in front of the establishments.

"Now, what?" I asked. "Where do you want Momma to go, Domino?" She'd stopped again and sniffed the ground whining a little. We bent down and saw a small dark smear.

"That could be blood," Neely suggested. Domino tugged on her leash and moved forward on the sidewalk leading toward the street. When we reached the curb, she grew more excited, moving back and forth a few feet. On the curb, not far from a parking meter, I bent down to see two drops of what appeared to be dried blood.

"More blood," I said, scanning the area around us. Still early, the street wasn't packed, but the traffic was steady. "Elizabeth must have gotten into a car parked here. I can't believe no one called the police about a bleeding woman being dragged all the way up the boardwalk and then forced into a car."

"There might not have been many people around. Unless she was screaming or making a huge fuss, it's possible no one noticed."

"Midge said it wasn't much blood, which is why she hoped she'd be okay if we could find her soon." Marty lowered her voice before going on. "When we first arrived at her room, the door was open a little. When we went in and found that mess, Midge checked the mattress lying on the floor. She said it was still warm, so she couldn't have been gone long. We figured she'd just gotten up and let someone into the room since the lock on the door wasn't broken."

"So, that must have been less than an hour ago. Do you see a surveillance camera?" I asked, searching the street again.

"No, but this coffee shop would have been open by then. Let's see if anyone at the counter remembers seeing a car parked here when they arrived."

"That's a great idea. You two go ask, and I'll wait here with Domino." Then on a hunch, I added. "Do you have that picture Charly sent us of Mark Viceroy, Neely?"

"Yes, I do. Ooh, that's an excellent suggestion!" She exclaimed even though I hadn't followed up my question with a suggestion at all. They returned in minutes with three coffees and a cup of water for Domino.

"One of the perky baristas told us she saw a pickup truck parked here. She remembered because it was a wreck and she wondered how it was even allowed on the road. Her equally buzzy associate at the counter said the 'old guy' she saw getting into it later could have been the same man in the photo I showed her on my phone," Neely said.

"And," Marty added, "she also said the woman with him was really drunk."

"Hm. Punch drunk, maybe, if Mark Viceroy worked her over trying to get her to hand over whatever he was after. It could have been the key we found inside the package or something with that lightning symbol on it."

"The surprises keep on coming, don't they? I'm sure Midge has her hands full with the police, but I'm going to call her. She needs to give them the information so they can speak to Ms. Perky and Ms. Buzzy." I dug into my bag and tried to find my phone.

"Why not? Midge already told me surprises, like misfortunes, seldom come alone. What's one more?" Marty asked.

"One more surprise or misfortune? Mark Viceroy seems to qualify as both," Neely observed.

"What will surprise me, is if the police take Midge seriously when she tries to convince them that Mark Viceroy's responsible for the destruction of hotel property and the possible abduction of Elizabeth Stockton," I added.

"Given Mark's reputation, the police can't be happy that he's out on the street and back in the area again. They don't have to take our word for it if they interview the baristas. If they don't already know where he lives, they must have some way to locate his home address sooner than we can," Marty assured us.

"Yeah, but if you were Mark Viceroy and you were holding Elizabeth Stockton against her will, would you stick around at any address the local police could dig up?" I asked.

"Let's hope he can't afford to miss his dialysis appointment and shows up later this afternoon. I'm almost certain that's still our best chance of catching up with him."

"I agree, Neely," I said just as Midge answered my call. I quickly gave her the details about where we were, the location of what looked like blood on the sidewalk and curb, and the information we'd obtained from the baristas in the coffee shop. I also mentioned the key and chain we'd found wrapped up in the scarf tucked inside the package.

"How's Midge holding up?" Marty asked as soon as I said goodbye.

"She says things are going 'as expected.' From her tone, I figure that means the police haven't swung into action. She also added that it's going to be a while before she can join us. She thinks we should go ahead and call Judith Rogow and Ginger Winger—Leonard Cohen's ex-wife—to warn them that Mark Viceroy's up to no good."

"So, Leonard Cohen has an ex-wife?" I asked.

"Yes, Midge got that information from another of her contacts before we tried to meet with Elizabeth. We hoped we could find out more about what, if anything, Leonard had to say to his ex-wife on his deathbed."

"Why did you suggest we meet for dinner at The Maiden Inn?" Neely asked.

"Midge says she and Marty picked up a rumor from her contacts in Santa Barbara that makes me want to have another chat with Nick Martinique. Let's hear what Marty has to say, but I'm pretty sure he was holding out on us." We both looked at Marty.

"Is she talking about what happened to Wendy Ballard?" I nodded.

14

Enemies

"Some people are nobody's enemies but their own."

—Oliver Twist

∞

"OKAY, BUT I need to drink my coffee. Do you want to go sit on the wall back there near the boardwalk?" Neely and I nodded as we all moved back to the sidewalk behind the coffee shop. One of the servers spotted us as Marty perched on the edge of a low wall with her back to the ocean.

"Hey, if you want to come in here and sit down to drink your coffee, dogs are allowed on the patio." Then she opened a low iron gate and ushered us to a table. Once we were seated, she left. "Holler if you need me to top off your coffee or bring you something else."

"Thanks," Marty said. The server gave us another smile and hurried inside. "It always pays to leave a good tip."

"She gave us a good one about the pickup truck," Neely retorted. "Who's going to call the ex-wives?"

"None of us know them," I offered.

"That won't matter if you can get the words 'Mark Viceroy' out before they can hang up," Neely said. "You and Judith hit it off. Call her and say, 'Hey Judith, it's Miriam, and I've got a recipe designed to save your neck.'"

"That doesn't sound like a joke to me. I'll try giving it to her straight. I've got Judith's number handy. Do you have one for Ginger Winger?" Marty nodded and began scrolling through items on her phone. My call to Judith went straight to her voicemail.

"Judith, this is Miriam Webster. I need to speak to you. It's important, so please call me as soon as you pick up this message." I ended the call, anxious about not being able to reach her. "I hope she's okay and not being held hostage by Mark Viceroy."

"I hope so, too. Here's the number I have for Ginger. Do you want to give her a try?" Judith was a busy woman, so I had no reason to believe she was in trouble just because she didn't answer her phone. My paranoia heightened my sense of urgency to reach them both ASAP.

"Sure—read it off to me." This time a woman answered my call on the first ring.

"Ms. Winger, this is Miriam Webster. I'm Judith Rogow's friend. I'm calling because I wanted to share some information with you about Mark Viceroy."

"Please, tell me he's dead." That caught me off guard.

"No, he's not dead. He's very much alive and in the area. We're concerned for your safety given a situation that's occurred here in Pismo Beach." Before going into the details about what had gone on this morning, I explained to Ginger that I was with a private detective agency Judith hired after hearing Leonard's claim that someone murdered her ex-husband.

"Okay, let me sit down, will you?"

"I don't want to scare you, but is your house secure?"

"Hang on, I'll set the alarm if that's what you mean. I live in a gated community that's patrolled by armed guards. If he turns up looking for me, he'll get more than he bargained for." The phone was quiet for a moment except for a rustling in the background. Then I heard what sounded like ice being dropped into a glass.

"Okay, the alarm's on, and I'm sitting down. What has that scoundrel done now?" I quickly explained what we knew at this point.

"I met Elizabeth Stockton when I visited Leonard. There's something flaky about her. I wish Leonard had just come right out and told me what he wanted Judith to know and I would have passed the message along to her. He was a sucker for a pretty face until the very end."

"When you say Elizabeth Stockton was flaky, what do you mean?"

"I don't want to badmouth nurses, but it has to be tempting to help yourself to whatever you need for a bad back or a bum knee. She had both, or so she said. On one occasion when I visited Leonard, I would have sworn that she was looped, and trust me, I know what I'm talking about." The tinkle of ice that followed made me believe her. "I wish Leonard had never met Mark Viceroy. That goes for Allen Rogow, too, although I don't believe it was his fault that he was mixed up with a loser like Mark Viceroy."

"Judith said much the same thing about his pal, Mark. Apparently, once an Army buddy, always an Army buddy."

"Leonard explained all that, but that didn't make it any better. Poor Leonard was so naïve. Even though he got into so much trouble using OPM."

"What's OPM?" I asked.

"Sorry, OPM is jargon in the finance business for 'other people's money.' He had no idea how difficult it would be to keep his clients happy. I know it's all water under the bridge now, and if your money's gone it's gone, but Leonard didn't start out intending to be a crook. He had a bad run of luck in the market, and when his clients started to bail, he panicked and broke the law hoping he could stay afloat long enough to fix the problem. Not that I knew any of this at the time. I guess that's hard to believe, isn't it—especially coming from a woman who married him?"

"Not for me," I replied without explaining about my own experience with a husband who I still hoped had never intended to be a crook.

"I apologize for going on about this, but Leonard's death has brought it all back for me. I would have stuck with him if his problems had only been about money. He was too easily led astray by women like Nurse Elizabeth, and his infidelity is what made me send him packing. Tell whoever's trying to track down Mark Viceroy and Elizabeth Stockton to be wary. I wouldn't turn my back on either one of them."

"Thanks for the advice. I'll pass it along. I apologize for adding to your burden so soon after Leonard's passing.

We're trying to round up Mark Viceroy, but I figured it was better to be safe than sorry when it comes to a man like him." I thought our conversation was ending. Then Ginger dropped a bomb—several of them, in fact.

"He's got to be too old to play Houdini anymore. What do I know? As old as he is, he still doesn't believe what I told him years ago. Once he left Vietnam, he wasn't just his own worst enemy—he was the only enemy in his life. At least until he turned into a mad dog." She paused and must have had another sip of her drink. "Given that Allen Rogow was serving time in prison for drugs, I thought that's how Mark Viceroy's troubles started, too. Leonard said no, that Mark had created big problems for Allen even while they were still in the Army together."

Be still my beating heart, I thought. I was eager to hear what she'd say next, so I spoke as calmly as I could.

"Did Leonard tell you what kind of problems Mark Viceroy caused for Allen in Vietnam?" Marty and Neely had already been staring at me, and their eyes widened. They were as big as saucers now.

"It had something to do with money and an operation that went south because Mark Viceroy became involved with a scheming civilian in Saigon. Apparently, Allen Rogow barely escaped with his life." Boom! Bomb number one exploded.

"It's a good thing Allen warned your husband about Mark Viceroy nearly getting Allen killed in Vietnam," I said.

"That's true. Even though Leonard tried to stay away from him, the guy still scared him. Mark had a hard time taking no for an answer even before Allen and Leonard were in The Men's Colony together." Boom! Went bomb number two.

"That's interesting. We took it for granted that Allen and Leonard met while they were inmates, but it sounds like you're saying they were already acquainted."

"Oh, yes, they became friends in an AA group. Booze was another of Leonard's weaknesses, but one he fought and eventually overcame. Leonard didn't like Mark after Allen confided in him, but it wasn't until they were in prison that Mark started to hound Leonard. Maybe Mark figured Allen couldn't constrain him from behind bars. Until Leonard refused to see him again, Mark pressured him to find someone to launder money for him." Boom! Boom! Boom! Bomb number three dropped.

"That was nervy," I commented.

"Gutsy, yes, but nutso, too, if you ask me. I mean, if Leonard was as connected as Mark Viceroy believed him to be, he wasn't a person you'd try to intimidate into doing something for you—especially when you barely know him. If Mark didn't regard Leonard as a man with powerful connections, then why ask him to do something illegal since Leonard obviously hadn't been clever enough to avoid prison? Even when Leonard got out of prison, the feds kept their eye on him. Like I said—nuts!"

"Was it drug money that Mark asked Leonard to launder for him?" Those wide eyes were staring at me again. Neely and Marty's mouths were hanging open now.

"I don't know how specific he got about where the money was coming from or how much there was, but he assured Leonard there'd be enough to make it worth his while. Leonard doubted Mark could have been making that kind of money from dealing. I agreed, especially given how much of his own product Mark appeared to be using."

"I understand what you're saying." I thought about what Wendy Ballard had told her brother, Nick, about the fact that Mark Viceroy was moving up in the drug dealing world. "Mark Viceroy must have had an inflated opinion of himself when it came to his role as a drug dealer, or he hoped Leonard could finance his aspirations to become a big wheel."

"He did throw some money my way trying to convince Leonard that he was a player. He showed up here with an envelope full of cash—thousands of dollars, I'm sure. Mark insisted that I accept it as seed money for a venture he was working on with my husband. I said no, thank you. He still wasn't happy even after I explained that Leonard was no longer my husband, that I'd never been involved in any of his business deals, and wasn't going to do so in the future. That only made him more insistent. It wasn't until I explained that I was still under surveillance by federal authorities that Mark finally went away."

"That was quick thinking," I said, wondering if I should have run a number like that on Jimmy Dunn. Federal agencies were involved in the aftermath of the Shakespeare Cottage affair, maybe I could have used that to make him go away. Not that it mattered anymore since he wasn't going to hustle me or anyone else ever again. "Did Leonard ask Allen what money Mark Viceroy was referring to?"

"Yes, and Allen was very upset when he heard about it, but his answer to Leonard was vague. Something like,

'It's blood money, and he's never going to get his hands on it.' Leonard and I figured he could have been talking about drug money or money related to the incident in Vietnam that nearly cost Allen his life." Once again, I thought we were winding things up and went into 'thank you' mode.

"This conversation has been eye-opening for me in so many ways. Helpful, too, so thank you. I hope I can call you back soon and tell you that the authorities have taken Mark Viceroy into custody."

"The sooner, the better and I hope they hang onto him. When we heard that they had Mark in jail and then let him get away, Leonard was beside himself for days. Leonard was out of prison by then, but what really irked him was when he learned that the young woman who visited Allen while they were in prison died not long before they arrested Mark. Leonard took her death hard because she'd approached him for money, hoping to get away from Mark. She was three sheets to the wind, but Leonard believed her when she said she intended to go to the police and tell them about Allen Rogow's murder and where they could find his body. He was sure Mark Viceroy was responsible for her death, one way or another." Boom! Boom! Boom! Boom!

"You must be talking about Wendy Ballard."

"Yes. That was her name. She had a fat lip at the time, so Leonard put her and that friend of hers on a bus to LA, along with cash for food and a place to stay."

"By friend, do you mean Nick Martinique?"

"Nick sounds right. I don't believe Leonard ever mentioned his last name. Leonard had to have been convinced Wendy was in imminent danger, or he wouldn't have risked giving cash to an addict."

"It's too bad he didn't take her straight to the police station," I muttered before I could stop myself.

"I agree. I didn't hear about it until after she died, but I told him that's what he should have done. The thought of going to the police made him physically ill when I urged him to go to the authorities even though she was already dead. He said no one would believe an ex-convict even if she was still alive. He was scared, too, about Mark getting away from the police. Leonard wondered if Mark and Allen were involved with special ops in Vietnam and Mark had government help to get away. It wasn't until they rearrested him years later and sent him to Calipatria, that Leonard gave up on his theory that Mark was in witness relocation or something like that. After the horror of that botched escape attempt in Calipatria, we both figured I was right when I'd pegged Mark as a cunning psychopath." She was quiet for a moment, and I heard that tinkling sound again.

How much can she be drinking this early in the day? I wondered. She didn't sound drunk, so maybe it was soda or orange juice.

"Miriam—you did say Miriam, didn't you?"

"Yes, that's right."

"My glass is empty, and I need to get a refill. Will you call me, please, the moment the police have arrested him?"

"I will. Promise."

"Thank you." When she'd gone, I worried all over again that I'd scared her unnecessarily. Then it occurred to me that if Mark was looking for a hideout, he might see older women, like Judith and Ginger, as people he could con or push around. I could imagine both women opening the door to him as a matter of decorum. In Judith's case, she might not be the least bit wary of Elizabeth Stockton if she turned up on her doorstep without any advance warning from us. I was about to call Judith again when she called me.

"Judith, thanks so much for calling me back so quickly. I wanted to make sure that you're aware of what's going on with Mark Viceroy."

"I know. He's been released."

"And already into more trouble," I added.

"How can that be? I was told that one reason he was paroled is that in addition to the fact that he's sixty-eight years old, he's suffering from advanced kidney disease. He needs a kidney transplant and had better get one soon, or he's not going to cause anyone any trouble ever again." Tick! Tick! I recognized another bomb about to blow.

"Is Mark Viceroy eligible for a kidney transplant?" When I asked that question, I wasn't specifically addressing Judith. Marty gave me a thumbs down sign.

"His status as a felon won't cause him to be denied a transplant. With his history of substance abuse, along with what must be a serious character disorder, he's a poor risk though. I'd bet the members of most transplant teams won't see him as a viable candidate. The regimen required for the transplant to be a success means playing strictly by the rules, which is something he may not be able to do even if his life depends on it. Charly probably knows the law better than I do, and your friend Midge would have a better idea about his chances from a medical standpoint. What's going on?"

"There's been an incident. We have reason to believe that Mark's involved, but we don't know that for certain. We think he's on the run, and he might have Leonard's nurse, Elizabeth Stockton, with him. We wanted you to know about it just in case he tries to look up old acquaintances in his search for a place to hide out. We don't want to worry you needlessly, but it's probably worth taking a few extra precautions for a day or two until the police catch up with him. I wouldn't be surprised if you get a call from Charly, too, just to make sure you're fully informed."

"I wonder why he went after Elizabeth Stockton, of all people. Maybe he's afraid Leonard told her something before he died that could put him back in prison. What she told me wasn't enough to do it. Do you suspect she withheld information about who killed Allen? How would Mark know about Leonard any of this?"

How, indeed? I wondered. *If Elizabeth Stockton was as flaky as Ginger claimed, could she have contacted Mark to sell him that key, or something else she picked up from Leonard?* Then I considered another option that seemed more plausible.

"Leonard's obituary was a matter of public record, and he was a celebrity of sorts, so maybe something about his 'deathbed confession' was leaked to the press. I don't believe we've come across anything like that." Neely shook her head no. "We have learned that rumors run rampant at the hospital where he died, and they were well aware of his infamy. If that's the case, Mark may have heard something that made him eager to speak to Elizabeth Stockton."

"I get it. I appreciate it, too. Thanks for emailing me the recipe, by the way. Maybe, I'll try it out while I'm waiting for you to put that guy back behind bars where he belongs. Even with his age and health problems, I can't believe they let him go."

"I promise to call you as soon as I have an update for you."

"Thanks. In the meantime, I agree that it's better to be safe than sorry and I promise you that I'll stay on my toes. I'll see if I can find a photo taken when he was released and, give it to security personnel, so he doesn't get into the front door here in the complex where I live."

"That's a great idea. I have one I can send you that the DMV took when he got his driver's license."

"How bad off can he be if they issued him a new license? Please send me the photo."

"I'll send it to you the minute our call ends."

"Great! I'll print out a copy for myself so I can throw darts at it now that he's free and I'm under house arrest!" With that, we said goodbye. An instant later that photo was on its way to Judith.

"Tell us everything, while it's still fresh," Marty insisted.

"An excellent idea, since some of what I have to say ties into the discussion we still need to have about what happened to Wendy Ballard, according to hospital staff who still remember her."

15

On the Evidence

"Take nothing on its looks; take everything on evidence. There's no better rule."

—Great Expectations

∞

"THAT HOSPITAL THRIVES on gossip as if Alyssa Gardener, and the busybodies that hang out at her Potter Cottage worked there. All sorts of rumors were flying around that Wendy Ballard's overdose was no accident. I agree with Midge that no matter how things look, or are rumored to be, it's better to go with the evidence. Midge wasn't talking about us, though. She believes the police should have investigated Wendy Ballard's death more thoroughly than they did."

"Rumors won't get them to take a closer look now. Heck, it's hard enough to get them to act on the evidence when it's jumping up at them like a horse on two feet!" Neely said emphatically.

"Was there any evidence to back up the rumors?" I asked.

"One of Midge's nurse pals, who's retired now, says

she recalled the situation after all these years for two reasons. 'Wendy was a pretty girl with a pretty name,' as she put it. And when the results came back from blood tests run to determine what drug she'd taken, there were huge amounts of heroin and cocaine in her system. So much, in fact, that either drug could have killed her. They don't typically find levels that high when someone dies from an accidental overdose."

"Does that mean they suspected suicide?" I asked. Before Marty could respond, Neely jumped into the discussion.

"I hope not. Nick must blame himself since he told us he was leaning on Wendy to get off drugs."

"His sobbing was mixed in with tons of guilt," I said and then elaborated on what I meant by that for Marty.

"If she was caught between Mark Viceroy's never-ending party and Nick's newfound interest in sobriety, that could have been too much for her," Marty suggested. "That wouldn't have been her brother's fault."

"She was obviously in a crisis of some kind when she asked Leonard Cohen for help," I observed. "I don't know why Nick didn't tell us about that visit with Leonard, or about the fact that Mark Viceroy had assaulted her."

"True! If he wants to feel guilty about something, it ought to be about going with her to ask Leonard for money rather than insisting that she go to rehab or to the police. If they'd gone to the police, and Wendy told them Mark had murdered Allen, he could have been sent to prison long before he ended up there. A murder conviction might have kept him off the streets longer, too."

"I understand what you're saying, Neely," Marty said.

"Nick and Wendy were kids. They had to be terrified and who knows if the police would have believed a couple of addicts. At that time, as far as the police were concerned, Mark was a vet who'd been honorably discharged after serving his country, right?" Marty asked.

"Charly probably would have told us otherwise if his service record had said anything else. I don't know when he had his first run-in with the law about his drug use, but Charly's working on a timeline," I replied. "They were right to be scared since it couldn't have been too much longer before she turned up dead."

"That's my point, though. Assuming she could have led the police to the body of one of his Army buddies, they might have picked him up and held him for questioning while they investigated the allegations. Mark couldn't have killed Wendy while he was in police custody."

"If he remained there," I said.

"He was slippery as an eel, that's for sure," Neely commented. "I'd like to believe that the police would have kept a closer watch over a murder suspect than some guy they'd picked up for drug possession." I nodded, agreeing with Neely as I spoke again.

"I wonder if I should nudge Charly about getting the timeline to us. It would also help us to see how the timing of Wendy's death jives with what Charly told us about Mark paying her fine and getting her out of jail before she'd served her entire sentence for a DUI. If he got wind of the fact that she was talking about turning him in to the police, he had to get her out of there." Neely briefly explained what Charly had told us about the incident.

"Okay, let's say that's what happened—Mark gets

Wendy out of jail and injects her with enough drugs to kill her. Was there any evidence to suggest someone else administered the drugs?" I asked.

"In Midge's opinion, it would have been hard for her to remain conscious long enough to inject herself with that much dope. When she got to the ER, the needle wasn't with her. That would have had fingerprints on it. There were only a couple of older injection sites in addition to the one used to take the drugs that killed her. Midge says that was odd, too, for an addict binging on heroin and cocaine."

"The older injection sites make sense if she'd just spent a month in jail where she couldn't have been injecting any drugs," I argued.

"I find it impossible to believe there wasn't a police investigation. Why didn't Nick ask for an autopsy? How did she get to the ER? Did he bring her in?"

"Midge talked to half a dozen people who all said they didn't know how she got to the hospital in her condition. Someone said some guy dropped her off and left before they could ask him questions about what drugs she'd taken."

"That doesn't sound like something Nick would have done," I said.

"No, but it couldn't have been Mark either. If he was intent on murdering her, why take her to the ER?" Marty asked. "Nick eventually turned up, although we didn't know it was him. One of Midge's contacts she spoke to at the hospital told her that Wendy's brother showed up to claim her body and make burial arrangements for her. Midge and I didn't make the connection to Nick since no one used his name and we didn't know he was her brother. Most of the information that would have been useful as hard evidence, like the results of those blood tests, must be gone since she died so long ago."

"If anyone on the medical staff reported her death as suspicious or ordered an autopsy, wouldn't she have been sent to the morgue? In that case, Nick would have gone there to claim her rather than to the hospital, right?" I asked.

"Maybe that's what the person Midge spoke to was trying to say. Let's ask Midge if she can recall what the person said about Nick's role when we see her. Midge must be close to wrapping it up with the police," Marty said.

"Or why not just Nick? That's only one of the questions we have for him now that several of our conversations lead back to him," I argued.

"Yes, they do," Neely responded. "I don't see a reason to wait until dinner time, so let's talk to him now."

"Good idea," I said.

"He already knows who you are and you're our designated caller, give him a try," Marty urged.

"All right, but I'd rather be close enough to grab him by the shirt collar if he tries to run away. Here goes nothing!" I said. The phone rang and rang and rang. I kept expecting the call to go to voicemail like Judith's phone had done earlier. After it rang about a dozen times, I was ready to give up when a weak, raspy voice spoke to me.

"Hello, who is this? I could use a little help."

"This is Miriam Webster. Am I speaking to Nick Martinique?"

"Yes, it's Nick. Come give me a hand, please."

"Are you at work or at home?"

"Home."

"Are you hurt? Do you need me to call for an ambulance?"

"Yes, I'm hurt. No, I don't need an ambulance. I could have called 911 if I thought I was in that much trouble."

"Okay, Nick, hang on. My friends and I are on our way. Stay put."

"Don't worry, I'm not going anywhere."

"Hey, Nick, Neely's here, and she wants to speak to you. Tell her what's wrong." I handed the phone to Neely and told her to keep him talking.

"Marty, we need Midge, now. Call her and tell her to say goodbye to the police. Then she needs to go to her car. Unless the police insist that they stay, Joe and Carl should go with her." Marty was on it before I finished the last sentence.

"Midge, we've got a new situation on our hands. Nick Martinique is in trouble. Let me ask." Marty looked up at us.

"Midge wants to know what kind of trouble. Is Mark holding him hostage—should she bring the police?"

"Nick, our nurse friend wants to know if we should bring the police. Just say yes if Mark Viceroy is there, and you can't say more than that." Neely was quiet for a few seconds.

"No, but he could use a nurse. Mark paid him a visit and got in a few punches before Nick could get to his gun." Neely raised both eyebrows as she said that. Marty relayed the information to Midge and explained what we wanted her to do.

"Did Nick shoot him?" I whispered to Neely, hoping not to disrupt the conversation between Marty and Midge or miss it if Midge had another question for us.

"Nick, did you shoot Mark?" Neely shook her head no. "The gun wasn't loaded."

While Marty and Neely were still on the phone, we started walking back toward the hotel, using the sidewalk rather than slogging through the sand again. That's why I wanted Midge and the guys to meet us in the parking lot.

"Follow us," I said when we met up with them. Midge was standing beside her car in the same lot where we'd left Neely's car. Joe and Carl pulled up beside her as soon as we arrived. Neely checked on Nick one more time, told him we were on our way.

"I can't believe we didn't call Nick!" I groaned as Neely drove to Nick's house. "He's so close, that would have been the first place Mark went. It never occurred to me that he knew Nick was in the area or where he lived."

"Hey, we warned him at dinner last night. Maybe that's why he had a gun handy even if it didn't have any bullets in it," Neely responded.

"You could be right. How did Mark find out about him?"

"The same way we did. Maybe he went to The Maiden Inn first, and someone who felt sorry for the old man told him how to find Nick. Let's put that on the list of questions to ask Nick if you think it's important."

"Once we're sure he's okay," I said. "Then I guess what's more important to me is to find out if Mark still had Elizabeth with him and, if so, what condition she was in. Then, let's unleash Joe's bad cop and give Nick the third degree about the issues he neglected to share with us."

"You can do bad cop," Neely argued. "Joe and Carl need to stake out that clinic. The younger Mark Viceroy would have kicked that gun out of Nick's hands, and beat him to within an inch of his life once he discovered it wasn't loaded. He wasn't taking any chances on getting shot, which tells me he knows he's in bad shape."

"Not in such bad shape that he didn't punch the daylights out of Nick. I agree that Joe and Carl need to get to that clinic and sit there. No fooling around either. The moment he shows up, they need to call the police."

Neely signaled and then pulled up in front of Nick's house. As soon as the others parked behind us, we all ran for Nick's front door. I knocked and tried the door handle at the same time. The doorknob came off in my hand. Using a pocketknife, Joe had the door open in two seconds.

"Nick! We're here. Where are you?" Domino woofed and darted down the hallway. She was pawing at a door and had it open before we got there.

"In here," Nick said in a strained voice. When we bolted into his bedroom, I didn't see him. I stopped abruptly, and we had a pileup of people. Domino kept moving.

"We need to wire you up with some brake lights," Joe said. I didn't care. I was more concerned about what was going on with Nick.

"Nick, are you in here?" Domino's head popped up from the other side of the bed. She wiggled and yipped, and then she sniffed the air and darted into Nick's closet. She whined and dug like crazy at boxes and suitcases in there.

"Yes," Nick replied. I walked around the bed and came to another full stop.

"Ha! I was ready for you this time...what the heck?" Joe asked.

16

A Little Key

"A very little key will open a very heavy door."
—Hunted Down

∞

"NEELY SAID MARK beat you up. She didn't say he bent you into a pretzel."

"I told Miriam I needed help. This isn't funny. Can you please get me out of here?"

If Nick's face hadn't been as red as a beet, I might have found a little humor in his predicament. The skinny guy must have tried to squeeze under his bed, which apparently loosened the bed slats. When the mattress and box spring dropped, they pinned him to the floor. The gun and his phone lay on the floor nearby. I tried to imagine the sequence of events which resulted in this outcome without success. I assume, in his efforts to free himself, he'd worked his legs out sideways, so his head and feet were showing.

"I salute you for your flexibility, Mr. Martinique. Now, let's get you out from under there," Carl said. "Joe, where can we get the best leverage? Tell us what to do."

Joe placed each of us at strategic points and told us where to grip to get the best lift. Midge and Marty were to drag Nick out.

"On my order!" Joe hollered. I felt like our situation had suddenly morphed into a Monty Python skit as our little band of active adults once again gave new meaning to the concept. "Lift!"

"All clear!" Midge said as my arms reached the point that they felt like spaghetti. I tried to let my corner of the mattress and box set down easy, but I didn't quite succeed.

"Don't move, Nick!" Midge ordered.

"Sheesh! I'm glad it wasn't a king size bed," Neely said, stretching her back.

"Is he okay?" I asked.

"Nothing broken, so far," Midge replied. "Go to the kitchen and bring ice or a bag of peas from the freezer, please." When I ran back through the house, I noticed that someone had begun to search Nick's place. It hadn't been demolished, like the hotel room where Leonard's nurse had been staying. Mark must have decided to force Nick to give up the location of whatever he was intent on finding. I dumped a tray of ice into a dishtowel and dashed back to Nick's bedroom. Joe and Carl passed me in the hallway.

"Where are you going?"

"A rendezvous with destiny!" Carl said.

"Our work here is done. We've got a scumbag to catch!" Joe added. "Plus, we have to get food before we stake out the clinic."

"No good cop, no bad cop. Only real cops, promise?" I asked.

"Only real cops, promise. We don't want to be real angels," Joe assured me.

Just as I got to the door of Nick's bedroom, he came limping out with Neely and Marty supporting him. Midge and Domino were behind him.

"Nick needs to sit and elevate his leg. I'm going to get my kit from the car to clean him up properly. Take that ice from Miriam and keep it on your eye. Marty, get him a glass of water and a couple of aspirin. When I return, I want you to tell us what went on here." With that, Midge swept out of the house with her car keys in hand. We'd barely finished carrying out her directives when she came back into the house.

"We're going to need more ice," she announced. A young woman was with her.

"What's she doing in here? Is Mark still out there?" Nick asked as he tried to get up out of his seat. I restrained him. "Get my gun!"

"Meet Elizabeth Stockton. She says Mark's gone, but he shoved her out of the car as he left—after he started driving away." Her chin was scratched, and she was bleeding from bad scrapes on both knees. She held up her hands to show us they were skinned too. Her cheek was red and swollen.

"Cry me a river," Nick said. "She's his partner and was helping him search my house until he came up with the idea that it would be quicker to get me to find what he wanted. She stood there, watching Mark hit me repeatedly before I punched him and ran to get my gun. Call the police!"

"I'm sorry. I wasn't his partner. Not exactly." Then

she swayed as if she might faint. She was younger than I expected her to be.

Marty sat her down on the couch, set up an ottoman that had been turned upside down, and propped up her feet on it. Her knees looked even worse on display like that. Neely dashed into the kitchen and came back with more ice as Midge had asked.

"Face," Midge grunted as she handed the ice to Elizabeth. "Start talking."

"I'm an idiot. He's going to kill me, isn't he?" Neely handed her a paper towel as the tears started to fall.

A young idiot, I suddenly thought, feeling sorry for her as she sobbed.

"You picked the wrong guy to "not exactly" have as a partner!" Neely chided as I dabbed at Elizabeth's knees with a damp paper towel I'd taken from Neely.

"I'm in over my head in debts—way in. Credit cards, dental bills, my car needs to go in for repairs, and I'm behind in my rent. I'm going to get evicted."

"Your point is?" Neely asked, still not backing out of her tough-gal mode.

"Leonard told me stuff about something awful that happened years ago—before I was even born. I took notes for him and put them into letters for people. He told me to call them and pass the information along to them. I was really scared about some of it, but he gave me money that he kept in a shopping bag beside his bed."

"What was in the letters?" I asked.

"And to whom were they addressed?" Midge added, now hovering above her with both hands on her hips. Nick had grown quiet as a mouse as Midge cleaned up his scratches and scrapes, applying antiseptics and bandages, and who knows what else from her little black bag.

"One was to his ex-wife, one to Nick, and another to this woman, Judith Rogow. That letter was short, and, mostly, about the fact that her husband always loved her and didn't leave her. He was killed and then buried at a place I'd never heard of before. At first, I thought Leonard said it was Dunkin's Dune—you know like the donut shop." Neely rolled her eyes.

"Judith Rogow told us you spoke to her, but she never said anything about getting a letter from you." The tears started again, and she squirmed.

"That's because I never gave it to her," Elizabeth replied, wincing a little as I tried to get the grit out of the scrapes on her legs.

"Why not?" I asked.

"I thought there was stuff in the letter that people might pay for, and I could use the money to get back on my feet."

"Were you going to sell the information, or use it as blackmail?" She looked at Neely and shook her head.

"Not blackmail—that's against the law. The first thing that happened is that I figured this Wendy Ballard person would give me money if I gave the letter to her instead of giving it to Judith Rogow. Or I thought she might pay me to keep her name out of it. That's before I knew she was dead."

"What? You have information about my sister?" Nick asked.

"She's your sister? Oh, no..."

"Quit moaning and groaning and spit it out. What

would Wendy Ballard have paid for if she hadn't died?" Midge demanded to know.

"Leonard wanted Allen Rogow's ex-wife to know that Wendy Ballard killed him, and then Mark Viceroy helped her bury him in that Dunkin' Dunes place."

"For goodness' sake, it's Dickens', not Dunkin's," Neely snapped.

"I know, I know. Leonard made sure I got it right. I'm just stressed out of my mind right now." I could believe that by the wild look in her eyes.

"How did Leonard Cohen know what happened? Was he there, too?" I asked.

"No. He said Wendy came to him for money and told him what had happened. She said it was a horrible accident—that Allen and Mark were fighting, and she tried to stop them. When she got in the way, Allen told her to beat it and that he didn't need her help and never would. She got so angry, she shoved him, and he went off a ledge or something, and when he stopped falling, he was dead. Mark helped her, but he threatened her after that and tried to force her to marry him. The way Leonard talked about it was like a weird soap opera. He called it a terrible midsummer night's dream. It was more like a nightmare if you ask me. She loved this Allen guy, he loved his ex-wife, and Mark loved Wendy. Like I said, weird." As she spoke, Nick had begun to cry again.

"I'm sorry your sister killed someone. I told you she didn't mean to do it. That Mark guy threatened her all the time by saying if she left him, he'd turn her over to the police, and show them where the body was buried. Leonard gave her money and she tried to get away, but I guess that didn't work out because he said she called him from jail a few days later. He thought she was better off in jail, but then she got out again. You should know better than I do what happened after that, Nick."

"Yes," Nick replied. "We rented a car with the money Leonard gave us, and we were going to go to Vegas, but then we stopped for a drink, and that turned into a few. Then Wendy bought pills. We were bigger idiots than you, Elizabeth. We got in the car and only drove a few blocks before she rear-ended someone stopped at a red light. She was lucky not to have killed the driver as hard as she hit the car. By then, that might not have mattered much to her anymore since you say she'd already killed Allen."

"Mark Viceroy also was mixed up in what happened to Allen Rogow, I thought he'd pay me to give him the letters. I was also supposed to pass along something Wendy left with Leonard for safekeeping, but I thought I could sell that to Mark Viceroy, too. He didn't much care about anything that was in those letters, but he was gung-ho to make a deal when I told him about a package Wendy had left with Leonard that I was supposed to give to a guy named Nick."

"So, where is it?" Nick asked.

"I already told you, I'm an idiot, Nick. I lost it. Mark didn't believe me. He thought I was holding out on him, and he totaled my hotel room looking for it. Then, he figured I'd double-crossed him and given it to you. That's why he came here once he found out where you lived."

"What was Mark looking for?" I asked although I figured we already had at least part of the answer to that question.

"A little key." Neely and Marty gasped.

"A little key to what?"

"Money. A whole lot of money. He needs it bad, too, because he's going to buy a kidney. I felt bad for him until he hurt me. You did a good job fighting him off, Nick. He's on medication to keep him going while he waits for a kidney. Until that happens, he can't miss his dialysis treatments or get badly hurt."

"Did he say where the money was?" I asked.

"No, but he drew this picture of lightning inside a funny shape and asked if I'd seen it, or if Leonard had told me where to find something with that mark on it. I told him, no. That made him mad, he tore up the picture, and shoved me out of the way. I fell and cut my arm on a piece of glass. That's when he got the idea of paying Nick a visit. He hit me hard, and after that I went with him without a fight, even though I was so scared I felt sick."

"Nick, do you know what a key like that might fit?"

"No, but I have a ton of stuff Wendy left behind in her room at the apartment where we were staying. I figured Mark killed her and was coming for me next, so I shoved all our stuff into storage at a cousin's house and left it there until I came back years later. I've never had the heart to go through it. Since that maniac wants it so much, I should put it in the dumpster at The Maiden Inn."

"Are you talking about the stuff in your closet?" Nick nodded. I spoke excitedly to everyone.

"You know what? I think the scent Domino detected on the scarf was Wendy's, not Elizabeth's. That must be the reason Domino was so interested in what was in Nick's closet when we got here." Domino had been lying quietly in a corner until I spoke her name. I pulled out the key we'd found earlier from the envelope I'd stuffed into my purse.

"That's it—that's the package I lost. How did you get it?" Elizabeth asked.

"Explain it to her, will you, Midge? Nick, I think it's time to go through that stuff in case the key fits something in there," I said.

"Go for it!" He said as he nodded wearily.

Neely, Domino, and I hurried to Nick's bedroom, while Midge explained how they'd picked up the package at the nurse's station. Marty went to find a snack for Nick, who looked like he'd lost ten pounds since we'd seen him the night before. Domino beat us to the room and by the time we caught up with her, she'd started pawing at the items in the closet.

"It's okay, Domino, we've got the message. Sit!" She did as I asked, and Neely and I began hauling items out of the closet. There were several suitcases with locks on them, but the key didn't fit. We opened each suitcase, and in an overnight bag, we found a letter addressed to Nick. The boxes were full of odds and ends, but nothing with a lock that matched the key.

"ATR—do you know what Allen's middle name was?" Neely muttered as she examined a monogram on a bag in the closet.

"No, I don't believe anyone's ever mentioned it to us. That could be his initials though, couldn't it?"

"Yep! This old thing has seen better days." Neely said as she struggled to drag an enormous scarred up old suitcase out of the closet and opened it. It was loaded with men's clothing including army fatigues, boots, books, and a framed picture of a young, happy Allen with his bride, Judith. We carefully searched it, but there wasn't anything inside that had a lock on it.

"We should to take this stuff to Judith," I said. "These things belong to her, not to Nick."

"You won't get any argument from me about it," Neely said.

"Let's put Wendy's stuff away. Then let me help you haul that suitcase out to the living room. We'll give the letter to Nick, and then tell him we're taking Allen's bag to Judith."

"Agreed," Neely said. Together, we put everything back into the closet—except for Allen's suitcase. We lugged that thing to the front door. It sure was heavy or maybe my arms hadn't recovered from lifting that mattress and box spring. Nick and Elizabeth, cleaned up and bandaged, were eating ice cream.

"Did you find a million dollars?" Nick asked.

"No." I felt disappointed since I was convinced that we'd solved the mystery of the "blood money" that Mark and Allen were fighting over.

"I didn't think so. Mark is off his rocker—he always has been." Nick scowled as if he had a bad taste in his mouth.

"We did find a suitcase that belonged to Allen, and we're going to take it with us for Judith. It should have been given to her long ago." Nick nodded.

"You're right. I'm not sure how Allen's bag got into her room. I was too scared and in too big a hurry to ask anyone about anything, so I put it all into storage."

"This was in Wendy's overnight bag. It's addressed to you." I took the empty ice cream bowl from Nick. His hand shook as he took the letter from me. As he read it, the tears flowed.

"It's a confession and directions to where she and Mark Viceroy buried Allen. I swear to you that I didn't know any of this. She was going to go to the police as soon as we got far enough away from Mark. We thought Vegas would work, and then she was arrested for a DUI. By the time she wrote this letter, she was out of jail; and she said if anything happened to her, to tell the police Mark Viceroy murdered her. He wanted her to marry him so she couldn't testify against him in court. When she refused, he hit her and threatened to kill her, so Wendy said it was only a matter of time."

"I'm sorry, Nick. She was an idiot, too, wasn't she?" Elizabeth asked. "Why didn't she go to the police?"

"The same reason I didn't go—we were afraid of the police and Mark. Why would the police believe us or protect us from him?"

"I get it." Elizabeth stood up, a little unsteady on her feet, and pulled a throw from the back of the couch where she'd been sitting. Then, she covered Nick with it. "He's shaking like a leaf."

"What's going to happen to Elizabeth?" Nick asked sadly.

"I guess it depends. Do you want us to have her arrested?" Midge asked.

"For what? Being an idiot? She didn't assault me. She can't be much older than Wendy was when she died."

"She helped mess up your place," Marty added.

"I'm sorry, Nick. I'll clean it up," Elizabeth offered. "The police will want to talk to me about what happened in my hotel room, though, won't they?"

"Oh, yes. You should speak to a lawyer first." I saw terror in her eyes. "Don't worry, I heard what you said about not having any money. Let me call Judith Rogow and ask her who to call to handle your case pro bono, as in free."

"Thank you. Would she do that for me after what I did to her?"

"I think so. She's got a big heart, which is why, after all these years, she still cares so much about an ex-husband who disappeared before you were born."

"Elizabeth's heart was in the right place and her head was on straight when she decided to be a nurse. If she can get out of the fix that she's in, I think she deserves another chance—one that Wendy never had." I nodded in response to Nick's plea, and then called Judith.

A couple of hours later, we dragged ourselves back to the resort. While Elizabeth tried to clean up some of the mess, the four of us put Nick's bed back together. Then we helped clean up most of the mess Mark and Elizabeth had created. Nick called a locksmith to repair the door and reinforce it. Judith was moved to tears when I told her we'd found some of Allen's belongings and a written confession from Wendy. She planned to come by our suite the next morning to pick up the suitcase and a copy of the letter Wendy had left for Nick years and years ago.

Before we left, a lawyer had arrived to speak to Elizabeth. She agreed to meet with the police if she could stay at Nick's place to make sure he was going to be okay. It wasn't until the police showed up that we left. Neely and I talked Marty and Midge into coming up to our suite for an early dinner and a soak in the hot tub to soothe our sore muscles.

"Gift card!" Neely said. "New bathing suits are on the house." They wearily agreed as we got into the elevator.

Even the best-laid schemes of mice and men often go awry. That's not a Dickens quote, but it **should have been.**

17

The Rules of Vengeance

"Vengeance and retribution require a long time; it is the rule."

—A Tale of Two Cities

∞

AS SOON AS we put the keycard in the lock, the door to our suite opened. Once I got over my surprise at seeing Charly standing there, I knew by the look on her face that we were in trouble. When Mark Viceroy jerked her out of the way and directed us all into the room using his gun as an invitation, I began to look for a way to escape. We clearly had him outnumbered. Joe and Carl were sitting on the couch like two kids who'd been sent to the principal's office.

"We had him under surveillance, but as soon as he finished his dialysis, he sneaked up on us from behind."

"I spotted these two dummies on my way in, and my plan was to lose them when I left the clinic. Unfortunately, one of you yahoos told the police where I was going to be this afternoon. Fortunately for me, they weren't any better at stakeouts than these two. I'm not sure what I would have done if you guys hadn't been sitting there with the motor running in my getaway car." Then he closed the door behind us.

"Sit down and get comfy. We're going to have a little chat, and when it gets dark, one of you is going to order the valet to bring around a car. Then we're going to go to Santa Barbara General Hospital to pick up a package that someone was supposed to deliver to me earlier today."

I was about to tell him that wouldn't be necessary, but I had a small task to complete first. No way would I give him the key that Wendy had left, but I figured I could switch it with a key that I'd taken from the suitcase that belonged to Allen Rogow.

"I don't want to cause you any problems, but I need to use the bathroom before it's too late." I was wired and jittery, so it was easy to do the little "gotta-go" dance. He nodded toward the bathroom I was supposed to use.

"Pull anything, and the dog gets it," Domino, who had been remarkably well-behaved, growled.

"It's okay, Domino. Momma will be right back. Go get your treats!" She didn't budge, and the poor little thing hadn't had much to eat since this morning. I gave up and slipped into the bathroom, switched the keys on the chain that Wendy had left with Leonard for safekeeping, flushed the toilet and then ran the water.

"That's a relief!" I said and then sat down. I looked at Midge as I spoke. "Midge, he can't possibly be talking about the package the kooky nurse left behind, can he?" I winked, and a light bulb must have gone off as a glint appeared in Midge's eyes.

"I doubt it. What are the odds that he's after her,

too?"

"You aren't talking about Elizabeth Stockton, are you?" Mark asked.

"As a matter of fact, we are. Does Elizabeth Stockton owe you money?" I asked. His eyes narrowed as he spoke again.

"Who are you people?"

"Grand Old Lady Detectives," Charly said and held out a business card that he took. Then, Midge picked up the conversation as if we'd rehearsed this entire scene.

"That young woman has run up bills all over the area. The police are after her for passing bad checks, but we'd like to get our client's property back without bringing in the law. She seems to have helped herself to something of great value for which the provenance isn't well-established."

"That's pricy stolen goods to you, pal," Joe said. Confusion reigned as a dozen expressions flitted through Mark's eyes and across his face. I didn't want to lose sight of the fact that this was a man who could beat people to a pulp, but he appeared lost. Then a shrewd look returned to his face.

"Why were you following me?"

"Because we saw Elizabeth Stockton get into a pickup truck with you earlier today. We figured you could take us to the location of the, um, missing item."

"What was the hooey about did I know the kooky nurse if you already saw her with me?" He was lost again. As he stood there, bumfuzzled, I noticed that he was inches from the ottoman that he must have been sitting on before we arrived.

"Let's just say it was a test of sorts. His body language looked okay to me, didn't it to you, Neely?"

"Oh, yes, and there was no indication that he was lying—I was tracking his eye movements very carefully."

"Where is it?" I asked.

"What?" He asked, with some irritation.

"How about we make a swap. I hand over the package Elizabeth Stockton promised to give you, and you tell us where she's taken the silver-rimmed, turn of the century biscotti crystal bowl that once belonged to Her Highness Princess Wilhelmina De Borgia?" His eyes were almost twitching, now, as I described a large fruit bowl sitting on the counter at Nick's house next to a box of biscotti. All of it was gibberish, but I was trying to keep him off kilter, waiting for a moment to strike.

To be honest, if he hadn't been holding that gun, I probably wouldn't have had the guts to do what I did next. He had to be worse off than Nick was. From all we'd learned about Mark Viceroy, he was one of the more despicable people I'd ever run into—since yesterday anyway. Still, I didn't want to kill him.

"As a gesture of goodwill, I'm going to let you examine the package we picked up while we were in Santa Barbara yesterday." I stood and reached into my bag.

"Slow down. Don't make me shoot you."

And bring twenty people down on your fool head, I thought.

"Trust me, I don't need a gun to put you down any time I want." Before he could even try to figure out that one, I slid my purse off my shoulder and opened it wide so he could see the envelope. Then, we got the knock on the door I'd been waiting for. I had no idea it would take so long. When Mark Viceroy aimed that gun at the door instead of one of us, I lunged. Domino did, too. I slung my bag and hit him with it like it was the biggest kubotan ever made! Domino rabbit-punched him in the gut, and he fell backward, tumbling end over end after he tripped over the ottoman. The gun flew, of course, and Joe scrambled to get it.

"Ah, another day, another gun. An Angel's work is never done!"

"The words of a true poet," Carl said.

There was another knock on the door. Charly opened it and a big guy in a sharp-looking suit followed a hotel staff member as he rolled the luggage cart into the room with Allen Rogow's suitcase on it. Ricardo Cantinela was right behind him.

"Cara Mia," he said. "May I give you a hand?" When I'd slammed my bag into Mark, and he'd fallen backward, I was propelled forward and landed with an oomph, face first, on the ottoman. It was softer than I'd imagined, and for a few seconds, I was tempted to stay there. As a result, I was still trying to push myself up when our visitors barged in, and the new disturbance began.

"No, thank you. I'm up!" I caught sight of myself in the mirror. My hair was standing up on end. Wouldn't you know it, Hank waltzed in. He motioned to a uniformed officer with him to get Mark.

"Cuff him, and read him his rights," Hank said.

"We have a few questions for him first," Ricardo Cantinela argued.

"I'm afraid you'll have to get in line," Hank replied.

"I've got top jurisdiction right now because he's wanted in Santa Barbara County for the murder of Wendy Ballard, as an accessory after the fact in the murder of Allen Rogow, and a dozen other charges."

"And so, we will wait." Ricardo apologized for the intrusion and excused himself. Before he left, he took my hand and kissed it in Continental fashion.

"Until we meet again, Miriam Webster. It's a relief to know you weren't mixed up with a man like Mark Viceroy. We've had our eyes on him for a very long time. You had me worried when you and your friends began to seek him out and then dragged an old suitcase that we'd also been looking for from a house so soon after Mark Viceroy left it. Forgive me, please, for my suspicions. I hope the note I sent with the candy and flowers makes up for it." Then he was gone.

"What's in this thing?" Joe asked as he removed Allen's suitcase from the cart. "Is it lined with lead or something?"

"Or something," I said as I flew into action. "False bottom." Neely got it instantly and emptied Allen's belongings onto the cart. She lifted a layer of fabric and cardboard like you'd find in any suitcase. Beneath it was a flat metal container that fit perfectly into the bottom of the suitcase. The tiny key I'd pulled from my purse opened it in an instant.

"Well, how do you like that?" I asked as I stared at money—not a currency I recognized. "I leaned in for a closer look. "Whew! French francs and not Italian Lira—I was afraid this was mob money."

"No, that's not what Ricardo wanted," Charly commented. The next round of visitors didn't even knock. The police officer who'd escorted Mark Viceroy from the room had apparently left the door unlatched.

"U.S. Treasury. Where is it?" Charly pointed to where Neely and I were still bent over the suitcase.

"There, Harold. Hold your horses, will you?" Then she put on latex gloves and knelt beside the suitcase. Very carefully, she lifted plastic wrapped sheets of money from the tray built into the suitcase. "Excellent counterfeits!"

"Are those counterfeiters' plates?" I asked when I saw what lay beneath the money.

"Yes," Charly replied.

"Why does anyone want them back? Are they still good?" Neely asked.

"No, but they tell a story that can convict members of the counterfeiting syndicate who are still alive and maybe lead to a newer generation of currency counterfeiters. Ricardo's pals would like to get their hands on this," Charly said as she pulled out a slip of paper. "It's the names of those who helped Allen Rogow get these plates out of the country before they could fall into the hands of the North Vietnamese. Once the operation fell apart, everyone assumed all of this had been lost. There was reason to believe that someone higher up was involved when the operation unraveled, and Allen was shot during an ambush. My guess is that Allen never knew for sure who he could trust after that with the mob also involved, and the possibility that his Army buddy had betrayed him. I'm sure he was still at a loss about what to do once he hauled this back to California with him a year later. If he'd lived a little longer, he might have figured out what to do with it."

"Mark must have been convinced Allen had the money, but didn't know it was counterfeit," I suggested.

"That's possible," Harold responded. "We believe Mark Viceroy was in cahoots with a local civilian who was killed at the scene. Before he died, the gentleman said he needed money to get his family out of Vietnam, so he was under the impression the money was the real deal. He and Mark Viceroy had been acquaintances, but the thief died before he could name others who were in on the heist. Then the bag disappeared, and the case went cold."

"Allen must have tried to keep Mark away from the money without giving away the details of the operation in which he'd been involved. It was an act of stupidity on Mark's part to want to use the money since the counterfeiters were in bed with an international crime syndicate," Charly commented.

"Yeah, we passed Ricardo Cantinela as he was getting into the elevator. He told us he was next to speak to Mark Viceroy so we should 'get in line.' I'll bet they don't like waiting to hear what he has to say. We'd like a crack at him first, of course, now that he's in custody. Maybe he'll be in a talkative mood once he understands that a mob lawyer is in line to speak to him."

"*Vengeance and retribution require a long time; it is the rule,*" Midge said marveling at the desire of the mob to seek retribution toward those who betrayed them half a century ago.

"Dickens could have claimed that the rule pertains to truth, too," I added.

That's when I remembered that I hadn't had the chance

to ask Charly to explain what she and the others were doing at our resort—not that I wasn't delighted about it. Even as the shadow of his former self, Mark might have figured out a way to exact a little more vengeance before we'd disarmed and disabled him.

"You called me, and I called everybody," Charly said in response to my question.

While we were still at Nick's house, I'd called her. As she explained it to us now, she'd been working on uncovering Allen's backstory about the operation in Vietnam. Once I told her about that suitcase, she remembered seeing a photo in the file that fit the description I'd given her. In two minutes, she'd realized its potential value and called her friend at the Treasury Department.

She'd also called Hank and told him about the written confession from Wendy Ballard and urged him to get to San Luis Obispo and stake his claim on Mark Viceroy. She figured the local police would already have him in custody. Then she drove to our resort hoping to meet us when we returned with Allen's bag.

"I was interviewing the woman who was with Jimmy Dunn at Dickens' Dune. It took her a day to work up her courage, but she came to report that something wasn't right about a man she met while hiking. She took off, and then couldn't stop worrying about the woman with a Dalmatian on the trail ahead of them. Anyway, once Charly called, I had someone else finish taking her statement. When we got to town and learned that Mark Viceroy had eluded the police at the clinic, we came here to warn you. I should scold you about the risks you took, but what good would it do?" Hank said, and then looked at me. "I'm glad you're all okay. What would I do with my free time if you weren't around to stir up trouble and keep life interesting?" I smiled as I met his gaze. Harold must have had enough of the chit chat and made his pitch to take possession of the items we'd found in the bottom of the suitcase.

In the end, the prize went to the representatives from the U.S. Treasury. They pulled rank on Hank and claimed that the contents of Allen Rogow's suitcase wouldn't have any bearing on any case he'd pursue against Mark Viceroy in California. They removed the metal box from the bottom of the suitcase and left the rest for Judith Rogow. This time when we put all his stuff back in it, I noticed a badge with the lightning symbol on a tag hanging from the handle of the suitcase. I pointed it out to Midge who nodded.

"That's the one I was talking about when we were in Elizabeth's hotel room."

"You should take a look at this, Miriam," Joe said, handing me the note delivered with the candy. Even though Ricardo was long gone, I still felt uneasy about opening it. That could have been because about a dozen people were staring at me. When I pulled out the sheet of paper that was folded up inside, I had to laugh as I held it up.

"Push me over with a feather!" Neely exclaimed. This copy of the phony promissory note was stamped in big red letters: PAID IN FULL. There was a little handwritten note with it.

"Please excuse the ill-mannered way in which Jimmy Dunn approached you. He overreached the

authority of the position he held and betrayed his employer's trust. It won't happen again."

Ricardo had that right. In that moment, I hoped I'd seen the last of the handsome, well-mannered lawyer. The only handsome, blue-eyed man I wanted to see again was standing in the room. I caught Hank gazing at me and gave him a smile that I hoped conveyed the gratitude I felt that he'd made my life more interesting, too.

Even though we had a lovely evening celebrating the fact that we'd done what Judith had asked us to do, I didn't really feel as if we'd closed the case until we attended a burial ceremony for Allen several weeks later. Hank and I had become an "item," after we showed up at the Sheriff's Department fundraiser together. He stood at my side as we watched Judith and her children place Allen in his final resting place. The Army had sent a letter of commendation in gratitude for his role in keeping those plates out of the wrong hands, although they didn't mention the specifics of the operation. They arranged to bury him with military honors for extraordinary service to his country. Charly must have had a hand in making sure Allen got the recognition he deserved.

After the ceremony, the ever-gracious Judith thanked us all for making the ceremony possible. Then, she noticed that Nick Martinique and Elizabeth Stockton were standing some distance away, watching the ceremony. That may have had something to do with the fact that they weren't alone. Apparently, Fleck had found a new home. I was overjoyed since I hadn't heard the news. I'd asked Denver Clemons to see if the foster parent thought Nick was a good fit to adopt the big guy. I was also touched when Judith embraced Nick and Elizabeth as if all was forgiven.

Getting closure with law enforcement wasn't going to be as quick. Mark offered to come clean about all sorts of things in the hope of cutting a deal that might keep him alive and get him the kidney he needed. It was still too soon to know how well that would work out for him, or how much of what he had to say we'd ever hear. It was a relief that he was behind bars even in his greatly diminished state, although even the scariest psychopath can't escape the fact that, according to Dickens, *death is a mighty, universal truth*.

By then, we were up to our necks in several more investigations, although nothing as complex or far-reaching as those that had gone on at the Shakespeare Cottage or Dickens' Dune, but a little bit of quiet was a welcome relief. As so often happens, I had no way of knowing it was the calm before the storm.

~THE END~

THANK YOU!

Thanks for reading Grave Expectations on Dickens' Dune. I hope you'll take a minute to leave me a review on Amazon, Bookbub, and Goodreads! If you haven't read the first two books in the series, I'd like to invite you to check them out. What's next for G.O.L.D. and Charly's Angels?

In *A Fairway to Arms at Hemingway Hills Seaview Cottages Mystery #4*, there's big trouble at The Blue Haven Resort & Spa. One of Marty Monroe's old contacts at the resort begs G.O.L.D. for help after a mishap on the golf course at the exclusive Hemingway Hills Country Club. A man is killed during a heist when a cache of arms is stolen from the guards who patrol the private enclave. When they learn the identity of the murdered man, how can they say no?

RECIPES

Amish Tomato Pie

Serves 6-8

Ingredients

2 cups Bisquick or substitute*
1/2 cup milk
2-3 medium tomatoes, sliced
1 teaspoon fresh basil, chopped fine
1 teaspoon parsley, chopped fine
1/2 teaspoon thyme leaves, chopped fine
1/2 teaspoon oregano, chopped fine
1/2 teaspoon onion powder
1 teaspoon brown sugar
Salt and pepper to taste
1 cup mayonnaise
3/4 cup shredded cheddar cheese

Preparation

Preheat oven to 350 degrees F.

Mix Bisquick or the substitute and milk into a dough. Press the dough into the bottom of 9-inch pie pan.

Cover the crust with a layer of sliced tomatoes.

Combine herbs with sugar, salt, and pepper. Sprinkle evenly over the tomatoes.

Mix mayonnaise and cheddar cheese and then spread over the tomatoes and herbs.

Bake for 35-40 minutes until the pie is a golden, brown color.

*Bisquick substitute
2 cups all-purpose flour
3 teaspoons baking powder
1/2 teaspoon salt
2 tablespoons butter

Sift flour into a bowl and whisk in baking powder and salt until well-mixed. Cut butter into flour mixture using a pastry cutter until evenly combined.

Sour Cream Coffee Cake

12 3" X 3" servings

Ingredients

Filling/topping
1/3 cup brown sugar
1/4 cup granulated sugar
1 teaspoon ground cinnamon
1/3 cup finely chopped pecans or walnuts

Cake
1/2 cup butter
1 cup granulated sugar
2 large eggs
1 teaspoon vanilla extract
2 cups all-purpose flour
1/2 teaspoon baking soda
1 1/2 teaspoons baking powder
1/2 teaspoon salt
1 cup sour cream

Preparation

Preheat oven to 325 degrees F. Grease a 9" x 13" pan.

Blend all the ingredients for the filling/topping and set aside.

In a large bowl, cream butter and the sugars together. Add eggs one at a time and mix well. Add the vanilla and mix again.

In a separate bowl, sift together the flour, baking soda, baking powder, and salt.

Add one-third of the dry mix to the wet mix and blend. Then add half of the sour cream and blend. Add another third of the dry ingredients and stir again. Add the rest of the sour cream, stir, and then add the remaining flour mixture. Blend everything one last time.

Pour half the batter into the prepared pan. Then use half of the filling/topping mixture to cover the batter. Add the rest of the batter to the pan and cover it with the remaining filling/topping mixture.

Bake for about 40 minutes—until the topping is brown and the cake begins to pull away from the sides of the pan. If in doubt, insert a toothpick and if it comes out clean, the cake is done.

Earl Grey Doughnuts with Brown Butter Glaze

6 Donuts

Ingredients

For the doughnuts

1/2 cup sparkling clear lemonade
1 teaspoon earl grey tea leaves
1 teaspoon vanilla bean paste or vanilla extract
2 1/4 cups all-purpose flour, plus extra for dusting
1/3 cup superfine sugar
2 teaspoons dry yeast
4 egg yolks
4 tablespoons unsalted butter, softened
1/4 cup heavy cream
2 tablespoons coffee sugar or Demerara sugar

For the brown butter glaze

3 tablespoons unsalted butter, chopped
2 cups confectioner's sugar, sifted
1/4 cup boiling water

Preparation

Place the lemonade, tea and vanilla in a small saucepan over medium heat until just warm. Place the flour, superfine sugar and yeast in the bowl of an electric mixer fitted with a dough hook and beat on medium speed until combined. Add the warm lemonade mixture and egg yolks and beat until just combined. Add the butter and cream and beat on medium speed for 6–8 minutes or until a smooth dough is formed. Place the dough in a lightly greased bowl, cover with a clean damp tea towel and set aside in a warm place for 1 hour–1 hour 30 minutes or until doubled in size.

Line a baking tray with parchment paper or use a silicon baking sheet. Roll out the dough on a lightly floured surface to about 1/2-inch thick. Using a 3.5-inch round cookie cutter, lightly dusted in flour, cut 6 rounds from the dough. Place on the tray, allowing room for them to spread. Using a 1.5-inch round cutter, lightly dusted in flour, cut and remove the center of each round. Set aside at room temperature for 30 minutes or until risen.

Preheat oven to 350 degrees F. Bake the doughnuts for 8–10 minutes or until golden brown and puffed.

While the doughnuts are baking, make the brown butter glaze. Place the butter in a small non-stick frying pan over medium heat and stir until melted. Cook for 3 minutes or until golden brown with a nutty fragrance. Transfer to a medium bowl, add the sugar and water and mix to combine.

Before the doughnuts cool completely, dip the top half of each doughnut into the glaze and place on a wire rack. Sprinkle with the demerara sugar and allow to stand for 10 minutes or until set, before serving.

Rainbow Antipasto Pasta Salad

Serves 10

Ingredients

1-pound dry rainbow rotini pasta
8 ounces diced Italian salami like Genoa, Calabrese, Napoli or Soppressata
8 ounces mozzarella, diced
8 ounces provolone cheese, diced
1 cup cherry tomatoes
1 can artichoke hearts,
1/2 cup each kalamata olives, pepperoncini peppers, & roasted red peppers.
1/2 small red onion, sliced thin

<u>Vinaigrette</u>

3/4 cup extra-virgin olive oil
1/4 cup red-wine vinegar
1 tablespoon fresh basil, chopped
1 teaspoon oregano—dried or fresh
1/2 teaspoon Kosher salt
1/2 teaspoon fresh ground black pepper
1 garlic clove, minced

Preparation

Cook the pasta in salty water according to package directions until al dente. Drain pasta and rinse under cold water for about 20-30 seconds.

In a large bowl, combine the cooked pasta and antipasto ingredients.

Whisk the vinaigrette ingredients together, pour over salad ingredients and combine. Serve immediately or cover and refrigerate—can be prepared a day or two in advance.

Barramundi with Pineapple Citrus Salsa

Serves 6

Ingredients

Fish

6 4-ounce portions of barramundi
1 1/2 tablespoons extra virgin olive oil
1 teaspoon sea salt
1 teaspoon black pepper
1 teaspoon paprika

Citrus Salsa

2 small oranges, mandarins, tangerines, or clementines peeled, segmented, and diced
1/4 cup fresh pineapple or pineapple chunks canned in its own juice
4 tablespoons fresh cilantro, minced
2 tablespoons fresh lime juice
2 garlic cloves, minced
2 tablespoons extra virgin olive oil
1/2 teaspoon sea salt
1/2 teaspoon black pepper
1/3 cup pomegranate seeds
1/4 small red onion, finely diced

Instructions

Fish

Preheat the broiler to high and adjust the oven rack 6 to 8 inches from the heat source.

Line a rimmed baking sheet with parchment paper and set aside.

Mix the oil, salt, pepper, and paprika together in a small bowl and place the fish filets onto the baking sheet.

Rub the fish filets with the marinade by hand or with a brush.

Broil fish for 8 minutes and set aside to lightly cool while preparing the salsa.

Pineapple Citrus Salsa

Using a small knife or paring knife, cut orange into segments, and dice. Add pineapple and mix.

Whisk together cilantro, lime juice, garlic, oil, salt and pepper. Stir in pomegranate seeds, onions and oranges.

Spoon the salsa over the fish and serve.

Crème Brûlée

Ingredients

2 cups heavy or light cream, or half-and-half
1 vanilla bean, split lengthwise, or 1 teaspoon vanilla extract
1/8 teaspoon salt
5 egg yolks
1/2 cup sugar, more for topping

Preparation

Preheat oven to 325 degrees F.

In a saucepan, combine cream, vanilla bean and salt and cook over low heat just until hot. Let sit for a few minutes, then discard vanilla bean or if using vanilla extract, add it now.

In a bowl, beat yolks and sugar together until light. Stir about a quarter of the cream into this mixture, then pour sugar-egg mixture into cream and stir.

Pour into four 6-ounce ramekins and place ramekins in a baking dish; fill dish with boiling water halfway up the sides of the ramekins. Bake for 30 to 40 minutes, or until centers are barely set. Cool completely. Refrigerate for several hours and up to a couple of days.

When ready to serve, top each custard with about a teaspoon of sugar in a thin layer. Place ramekins in a broiler 2 to 3 inches from heat source. Turn on broiler. Cook until sugar melts and browns or even blackens a bit, about 5 minutes. Serve within two hours.

ABOUT THE AUTHOR

An award-winning, USA Today and Wall Street Journal bestselling author, I hope you'll join me *snooping into life's mysteries with fun, fiction, and food—California style!*

Life is an extravaganza! Figuring out how to hang tough and make the most of the wild ride is the challenge. On my way to Oahu, to join the rock musician and high school drop-out I had married in Tijuana, I was nabbed as a runaway. Eventually, the police let me go, but the rock band broke up.

Retired now, I'm still married to the same sweet guy and live with him near Palm Springs, California. I write the Jessica Huntington Desert Cities Mystery series set here in the Coachella Valley, the Corsario Cove Cozy Mystery Series set along California's Central Coast, The Georgie Shaw Mystery series set in the OC, The Seaview Cottages Cozy Mystery Series set just north of the so-called American Riviera near Santa Barbara, and The Calla Lily Mystery series where the murder and mayhem take place in California's Wine Country. Won't you join me? Sign up at: desertcitiesmystery.com.

Made in the USA
Coppell, TX
02 July 2020